ONE AND A...

Downfall

When the westering summer sun shines into the low windows of the little fishing village, most people would agree with the motto on the bottom of the old hand-coloured postcards: "Cornwall: No better place in the world!" But in winter, braced for a storm, the dour, drenched facades of the cottages were more like death masks than welcoming, smiley faces.

Out on the cliff, alone by the fire in the White House, Lady Olivia Hawkins listened to the wind and the rain and the waves pounding at the foot of 'her' cliffs, 200 feet below and smiled, remembering that the weather on D-Day had been such as this but that had been in June more than seventy years ago, and today was February.

As the rain swept in off the Channel from an obscured horizon, bullying its way into the pub with the entering customer, a broad Birmingham accent cheerlessly repeated a regular joke. "Swat we cum down here for, loik , days loik these."

"Just a little Cornish mist" came the regular reply.

"Trouble is, it ain't missed- Oi'm drenched."

The first speaker whose Black Country tones were, if anything, broader when the weather was bad, shook what water he could from his flash Helly Hansen waterproof jacket and hung it on the coat hooks by the door of the *Coverlet Arms*, ensuring that the logo of the expensive waterproof was visible to all. However, you only had to look at the portly figure and well-fed jowls to know that he was no seaman. Ashley Pine took his accustomed stool. His apologetic friend, Henry Lake, was already *in situ* seated at the bar.

Henry owned the shop which struggled on pluckily in the face of the rising tide of incoming delivery vans from the four monster supermarkets and smiled enigmatically, a regular reaction, especially to his wife and two daughters; Ashley more than made up in verbosity for Henry's reticence.

"If I 'adn't known yow were coming out for one, I think I'd've stopped in." said Ashley.

"And there go the pigs , flying in neat formation across

the sky."came the repost from behind the bar.

"Cheeky'"

The beautiful girl in the black polo-shirt issued by the brewery backed up her remark with a stunning smile so that it was impossible to take any umbrage. Tegan Trembath had been away to the big city, or one of the big cities, whichever it was that had held the university that she hadn't liked at all and so was one of the best qualified barmaids in Cornwall. Classic Cornish good looks in which the Spanish blood from the survivors of the wrecked Armada was still evident more than four hundred years on were coupled with a very good brain. The only flaw in this recipe for spectacular success was the ingrained horror of cities and the lifestyle that they spawned. Eventually, some very lucky fisherman or boat builder was going be chosen as her mate but until then, at twenty three, she was very happy sharing the family cottage with her mother and , as a party piece, beating the calculator function on a mobile phone in adding up the cost of a round. Charlie Onions, the landlord of *the Coverlet Arms* was happy to pay her over the odds, partly because he knew quality when he saw it and partly because his roly-poly missus, Doris, told him to.

"Dun wanna lose a maid like she. Brings the few we still got left in the village out of a night like this."

'T*he Coverlet Arms*' , locally known as '*the Cover*', had taken over from the clutch of grog shops and kiddlywinks that had, many years ago, satisfied the needs of a population of boat makers, fishermen and deep-sea sailors that had lived in the village of Porthwallow since time immemorial. Though not mentioned in the Domesday book, neither were either of its neighbours, Fowey and Polperro. They had initially clung to the foreshore, like the very limpets that they ate along with other shell-fish, seaweed and gull's eggs; gradually their habitations, their food and their boats had become more substantial and men from the village had sailed to the Grand Banks in search of codfish years before Columbus or Cabot had bothered to look for dry land beyond. Their heydays had been in the Nineteenth and early Twentieth centuries when the china clay from the ground and the pilchards from the sea had made them rich. Sadly, both the natural treasures had been overexploited and virtually eradicated. At the height of that wealth, some ram-shackle net lofts that had stood on the quay had been replaced by '*the Coverlet Arms,'* and become one of the finest public houses in the Duchy , in a thriving summer holiday centre.

However, on a midweek winter's night like this, it was easy to believe that the whole place had been sold, lock, stock and tar barrel to the invisible oligarchs 'upcountry' who now owned almost all of the more desirable cottages near the water and who would arrive occasionally in their monstrous 4 by 4s, gleaming white with the new evil-grinning LED headlights . The young ladies of the village whom the new owners employed as cleaners would have been warned of the arrival in advance, so that they could make a pretence of activity and cleanliness, otherwise the visits would have been no more predictable than the weather forecast.

"Best way ter check the forecast", said Jago Hocking, local boatman, occasional builder's labourer and original wit, "be to look outa the windy."

Jago was 48 and, like Tegan, had been born in the village and been away but unlike Tegan, he had gone all the way round the world before coming home again. He had rid himself of the charming misuse of grammar that marked out the real Cornish but ,on return , was gradually allowing himself the luxury of slipping back, so as to avoid being taken for an incomer by those who had moved down during his vagrancy.

Jago had a stool at the far corner of the bar and many a visitor had been frozen by his icy blue stare when they had made the mistake of sitting there. That night, unsurprisingly, there were no visitors so Jago was, if not all sweetness and light, certainly displaying the natural charm that came so easily to him.

"And tis winter- us d'need a good storm- stir it all up a bit out there- fish've just been asleep on the bottom-"

"I know some people like that."

"What?"

"Asleep on their bottoms!" riposted Tegan.

"Sure they're not dead?" asked the shop-keeper Henry Lake, glumly. Wearing his trade-mark sloppy beige cardigan, he gazed into the bottom of .his glass. It was a specially worked glass, issued by the brewery for a special

brew. When the beer first came on the market, each of the pubs had been issued with half a dozen glasses and five had disappeared from *the Coverlet* within the week.
"Disgraceful!" Mr. Lake had said. "I wanted one of those."
"Dun' ee worry, Mr.Lake,"said Doris. " Us'll put one by, special."

"Dead? The fish? "asked Jago, "Only because bleddy Brussels has said to chuck back those as is over quota. Tis obscene.!"

"Immoral!" said Ashley Pine; he liked to consider himself a local and so agreed with almost everything Jago said.

"A hundred pound monk- thrown back dead or dying because some arsehole in Europe said so, 'd fetch two thousand quid when dressed, easy. Tis criminal. Now that's who I'd 'eve at the top of that list of yourn- they bleddy twats as makes up the Common Fisheries Policy."

"List?" asked Tegan. She was not so rabidly opposed to all things European and anyway, liked to know what the village was talking about.

Surprisingly, Henry broke into song: in a remarkable

capable tenor, he sang:

"As someday it may happen that a victim must be found
I've got as little list, I've got a little list
Of society offenders who might well be underground
And who never would be missed,
They'd none of them be missed."

There was a pause.

'The Mikado'? " he offered. Still blank faces so he tried a little further. "Gilbert and Sullivan?"

Heads shook.

"Bloody philistines!"

"You want to watch it- us Cornish has our own language!" Jago replied. And then, aside, "If only some bugger could understand 'en. And our literature! Writ on the back of shit-house doors. mostly!"

He went on: . " We was talkin' about a list of folks as we could well do without; starting with the Prime Minister. And that new president they got across the Pond"

"Are you taking the whole of both Houses of Parliament together? "asked Tegan, "I mean, if you took them individually you'd have a list of nearly fifteen hundred names! Just to start with."

"Fifteen hundred!?" Ashley actually sprayed his mouthful of beer across the bar. "Now, let's not exaggerate, girlie!"

Tegan handed him a bar towel so that he could mop himself down. She hated being called 'girlie', or for that matter, any condescending sexist label that this sort of dinosaur would come up with, but she would save her revenge for later. "There are eight hundred and five members of the House of Lords, for a start."

"Come on, now. I don't believe that for a moment.!"

Tegan took her phone from the tight back pocket of her jeans; she was one of the few, very fortunate girls for whom the boon of the contraception pill had not brought about the bane of the pear-shaped bum and strapping thighs. Stunning figures at seventeen so often broaden in the beam as they age but hers was not one; after a moment of blurred activity, all fingers and thumbs , she presented Ashley with the screen .

Ashley said: "I haven't got me readers..." and so Henry lent him his.

"I don't bel- " Then he realised that he was going to sound

like that Victor Meldrew from off the television and so stopped. " I bow to modern technology."

" Shall us just stick to the parish?" suggested Jago. "There's a dozen councillors there for a start as us could do well without."

"I say, "said Ashley, "Is that fair?" He had secret ambitions of being elected to the parish council in the none-too-distant future, more as a sign of being accepted into the community that in any philanthropic drive. In his eyes, it would rather like being invited to join the Masons.

Just then, a rare occurrence happened -the vicar entered.

"Vicar!" called Jago- "How the devil are you? You'm just in time. We were just discussing mortal sin- I seem to remember murder was a mortal one, rather than venial?!"

"Oh yes indeed-,"replied the Reverend Trevor Uphill." but may I just acquire a little-ah- refreshment? A bit out of breath- before giving a class in ethics, not to mention semantics. "

"So we won't," interrupted Tegan, "what can I do for you?" she asked, smiling beguilingly.

The vicar was one of the few men with whom she

conversed from her moderately defensive position behind the bar with whom she could be so provocative; normally it would evoke some mildly mechanical, rude retort of sexual ambition involving her and her superb physique but the vicar was, in the euphemisms of the village, either 'not that way inclined' or ,more recently, 'that way'. He had initially, twenty years ago, when he had first come to this parish, made no song and dance of his propensity but gradually, on the occasions when song and dance had been forthcoming, such as after the church fete or at Christmas, it had become more of a subject of conversation among the few fading spinsters of the congregation, that there was another good man wasted and when he had quietly installed Jeremy, a no-longer young man in the granny flat at the Vicarage as a welcome lodger helping the coffers with his rent and the parish with occasional voluntary secretarial work , no one was particularly surprised. The recent edicts from Lambeth Palace and absence of signs of bolts of lightning from on high in punishment for gay marriage of members of the clergy had put a noticeable spring in his sixty-year old step.

" V and T, dear- a large one-And looking at that sky, I wouldn't be surprised if they hadn't started knocking up an ark down at the yard. If they can find any gopher wood. I suppose you lot are all paired off , packed and ready to go? No, I mean it- I mean, we're very sheltered here but there a 'heller' of a storm coming in out of the West out there. I've lost track of which of those hurricanes the Yanks've just passed on to us. Irwin, is it?Yet another example of the bounty of our American cousins that we could well do without. "

After all those years, the vicar know 'a 'heller' when he saw-and heard one.

" Now, back to sin- my favourite" And he too, incongruously, perched at the bar". Well, Jago dear boy, I was going to be very simplistic and say that the mortal sins are the ones you probably haven't committed while the venial ones are the ones you're more than likely to have done- but then I thought that's not fair.

'Venial sins' are slight sins- like being naughty but not really wicked. If we gossip to such an extent as to destroy a fellow's reputation- that's mortal- like murder. Remember

Cassio in '*Othello*?"

The others looked blank, even Tegan.

"Sorry, I read 'Computing.'"she said, in some way explaining her ignorance.

" No ?- But if we just gossip in general, that's just venially sinful."

"So if you was Catholic, your confessional 'd be packed with venial sinners, the amount of gossip as goes on in this village!"said Jago," And they d' stop and do it in the street!"

"Well, you should know, lad- you're usually the subject of most of the tittle-tattle."

And that was when it struck.

The first they knew of it was a massive crash, as if the local giants of legend were still chucking rocks. Then they could hear the rain. Then the lights flickered and went out.

"Candles!"

The regular call showed that this was nothing new.

But then the very earth did quake, the like of which none of them -not even Jago Hocking when he had been out East- had experienced before.

A drenched fireman put his head round the door. "It's ' village 'all!" This one had moved recently down from Yorkshire and unlike many of the new incomers, had actually involved himself in the place. "Parking lot's washed 'alf way down 'ill. And village 'all an' all 's gone wi'it!"

It took a moment for them to realise that he meant the Village Hall.

"Brownies!" screamed the Vicar. " It's Tuesday. The Brownies meet of a Tuesday! In the Village Hall.!" "

And before anyone could stop him, he made a dash for the door of the pub and tried to run up the hill. It didn't take long for Jago to catch him and explain.

"They were disbanded."

"What!?" The shock seemed to have deprived the vicar of his understanding. "But every Tuesday since I can remember..."

"Disbanded. Only a handful of Rainbows, a couple of Beavers with special dispensation and a Brown Owl who's six month pregnant."

"Are you sure?"

"Yes-but it wasn't me.."

"No- about the Brownies..."

"Yes. The place would have been empty."

By now they had realised that the Fore Street was indeed becoming a river of the liquidised shale that that whole coast was built on and , indeed, seeing the shattered remains of the Men's Urinals floating down on top of it, they realised that there was nothing that anyone could do until the night had passed and the weather improved. By mutual silent consent, they returned to the pub.

As is only right, and in the absence of the Village Hall, the pub had once again become the social centre of the community. In all sorts of waterproofs and carrying an assortment of torches, the people were gathering for some sort of mutual reassurance, aided by alcohol.

"Wish it would rain more often," was all Doris had time to remark as she and Tegan rushed to minister to all the various cases of shock.

Some of the older ladies, brought up in the various Baptist or Methodist Non-conformist traditions that had once been so popular, felt that the disaster , if it was indeed an Act of God, temporarily freed them from their oaths of Temperance and so were making serious inroads into the ginger wine.

Even the children were being allowed 'something purely medicinal' and very soon the night was becoming something of a bacchanal, to be remembered, if not in detail, for a very long time.

Chapter 2

Daylight- the clear light of day- did make things a little clearer. There had indeed been no-one in the Hall and nobody hurt, although Mr. Pine's nearly-new white Land Rover Discovery had been caught up in the maelstrom and washed down the hill, reminiscent of the motor home in the Boscastle floods of '04.

"It's his own fault," Deirdre, his wife, complained to anyone who would listen when she went into the shop. " Lazy bugger. He drives down, parks outside the Hall and then walks the last bit. Pretends he's walked all the way. He's not supposed to park it there. More Divine justice."

And this indeed was going to be the problem; to what

extent was the landslip to be deemed an Act of God or the fault of the Water Board, or indeed of the electric people?

Even before the road had been cleared and access to the bottom of the hill re-established and with it the possibility for the dray to restock t*he Coverlet Arms* -who had had their best non-festive winter's night ever- even before that, the Committee had to be established: the Reconstruction Committee.

In the absence of the Hall and the obstruction of the pub, they were meeting in the dining room of Vincent House, by kind invitation of Lady Olivia Vincent herself.

"There are times," she had said to the Vicar, of whom she approved," times when one has to remember one's position in Society- or at least in the community, even if the community is no longer aware that one exists!"

Olivia Bolitho had married into the Vincent family after the War. On his father's death, Nicholas Vincent had been left the White House, part of the extensive but scattered Vincent estates, perched on the cliff with views down the Western Approaches towards Roseland and America beyond. The ignorant said that, on a clear day, they could see the Lizard but that would have involved X-ray eyes. The house was very obvious from the sea and indeed featured as 'white house conspicuous' on some charts.

Gradually, the cliff was being eaten away by the sea, some two hundred and fifty feet below and eventually the old house would no longer be there and there was a surreptitious book being made among the high-rollers of the village as to whether Lady Olivia would die before the house carried her off with it when it went.

Politics were involved in the establishment of the Reconstruction Committee; there were definitely those who ought to be on it, those who definitely ought not to be on it, those who thought they ought to be on it and those who wanted nothing to do with it. The demarcations were not obvious.

Lady Olivia had condescended to be a member and had chosen the title of 'Vice-President' for herself.

"I'm the sort of person whose name looks good on the letterheads of pleading missives." she had said. It meant that she could keep an ear on the fate of her beloved village without it being percolated through that universal purveyor of the local news, Dorothy Dingle. Mrs Dingle automatically and without really being aware of it, put a 'spin' on any story. which made it more colourful and perhaps less true than it actually was. She had single-handedly been responsible for several phantom pregnancies, a couple of broken marriages and the report of the sexual shenanigans of some of the most innocent youngsters in the village, rarely allowing fact to impinge upon her imagination. These were usually presented over a large cup of tea and half a packet of chocolate digestives at the table of the kitchen which she was nominally employed to clean.

Then, obviously, the Vicar. And where the Vicar went, Jeremy came as part of the package, so at least they has a secretary.

"How many of us should there be, Vicar?" asked Lady Olivia.

"Oh, at least a dozen, don't you think, Jerry?"who bowed mutely.

"Splendid! It has been an absolute age since I have had the dining table out to full stretch. The last time, I seem to remember, was when we laid out dear Nicholas on it."

"What happened?" asked Jeremy.

"Oh, he died, dear. He'd died."

"God rest his soul," said the Vicar, automatically crossing himself.

"Oh, I'm sure He has; there was nothing Nicholas ever did in this life that was likely to put his life hereafter in jeopardy. He was a very boring man. Did you know him?"

"I think he'd passed just before I came."

Jeremy had noticed a photo in a silver-gilt frame; a Guards officer in full uniform, laughing at the camera.

"Is this him? Very good-looking."

"No, dear" said Lady Olivia. "That is my Isaac. My son. My only son. He is laughing at the prospect of going off to some silly war just to keep that dreadful woman, Thatcher, in power. Put off his wedding until he got back. He died on Tumbledown"

"Oh, I- "

"Not to worry dear- you weren't to know-Thirty five years ago." She gazed for a long time at the photograph , then seemed to shake herself. " So. Who do we know that is useful?"

"My John."

The voice came from Dorothy in the doorway. Whether she just happened to be passing or had taken up her usual spot in earshot nut just out of sight whenever anyone came to call, no-one was sure. "Very useful, 'e d'be. 'round the 'house and that. And in the garden,"

"Thank you, dear,"said Lady Olivia, "but I think this is likely to be rather too big a job for your John. We shall need professionals- big companies- rather than amateurs, even ones as gifted as your |John."

"Suit yerselves," and Dorothy positive flounced out of sight, but no-one was very sure how far.

"Should we try to keep the numbers equal?"

"Between men and women, dear? I always think that sort of stuff is so much tommy rot. Everyone knows women are so much better than men in most areas but you have to admit, it, most builders one sees are men,. They have the bottoms for it."

"No," said the Vicar, "I was more thinking , on the committee, between-ah- indigenous and incomers. A far

wider rift than simply between men and women. The channels of communication are really very complicated."
"Oh, God,"said Lady Olivia, forgetting herself," Oh, sorry,dear but you know what I mean. The English invasion of Cornwall is one of our oldest bits of colonialism and still they won't let us forget it. We gave Rhodesia back to the locals and look what they have done with it. If we left Cornwall to the Cornish, they'd be back in the Dark Ages in no time.!"
"I 'eard that, yer ladyship"
Dorothy came in like a squall across the bay.
"Well, you weren't meant to but even you, dear, can't claim to be pure Cornish. Where was it your father came from?"
"Mother weren't sure but it was off one of they boats as has writing you can't read."
"She means Cyrillic script," explained the old lady." We used to have considerable business with the Baltic States, you know. Almost dried up now, of course, but there are a number of villagers with fathers from further afield than Polperro. Some even stayed and married."
"My mother was married!"said Dorothy," Just not to my

father, that was all."

While the establishment of the planning committee was being discussed in the White House, some more practical steps were being taken down in the village. Jago had called together a couple of the local builders, small, one- or two-man operations which made a very steady living converting the old fishermen's cottages according to the whims and fancies of the wives of the latest buyers from upcountry.

No matter how recently it had been done, the kitchens and bathrooms- at the very least- had to be ripped out and replaced. Sometimes the roofs were re-tiled, sometimes wood-burners installed , sometimes outhouses- the erstwhile lavatories- were rebuilt to accommodate the particular pass time of the new owner. They would employ their brothers-in-law or nephews as painters and decorators, next-door neighbours as electricians and the daughter's boy-friend who had done a course at Cornwall College as plumber and take it very ill if one of the new owners took it upon himself to hire someone from outside the village.

The three of them standing at the bottom of Fore Street,

looking at the desolation, made a fine display of Cornish manhood: Jago, slight and wiry, Nathan, monumental as if carved from a nearby granite tor ,built like the proverbial shit-houses that he spent half his life knocking down, and Hezekiah, known as 'H', more evidence if evidence were needed of the recent Non-Conformist past.

"Tis fucked." sad H.

"True,"said Jago," but not a great 'elp as evaluations go."

"Tis too much fer we," said Nathan.

"County's gonna 'ev to clear the shit an' rubble."

*Oh, I dunno," said H."I knows a man, mate o' mine, 'e'd let us 'ave a JCB at a very nice price- we could get that lot shifted 'afore they buggers even gets into work Monday."

"Naw!"

"We got to get it cleared-get a ambulance through, or you fire boys."He nodded in the direction of Nathan who was one of the retained firemen.

"They have a fire this side o' the slip, they'm buggered- never get through. And there's still one or two as lives downalong- old Mrs Tonkin fer a start."

They stopped as they heard an unusual noise-

"What the bloody' ell's that?"
Back up the hill, above the landslip, they could see the roof of some sort of vehicle-
"Hey, us shan't need your mate's JCB," called Jago, "Tis Steve off the farm. With what looks like 'is snow plough."

The big farmer matched Nathan in stature; they had made a formidable second-row for the local rugby team ten years ago; it had only been their apparent inability to comprehend the laws of physical conduct that had stopped them playing for the county and the club had earned, quite rightly, the reputation for being the dirtiest team on the circuit when either of them was playing.

He was gradually working his way down hill, forcing a way through the shale and slate, parting the flow like a Moses, not caring where the spoil went on either side as long as a way was cleared. Sadly, he cleared away the rubble that had been blocking the Village Hall's stop-cock, so a spray to equal the *manneken pis* was added to the flux; fortunately, any running water went straight into the sea, so it was a hindrance rather than a disaster.
"Careless bugger!" shouted Hezekiah.

"Snot my fault," yelled Steve. " I'd a thought anyone with a 'haporth of nous'd 'eve turned off the stop cock! What was Cuthbert, Dibble an' Grubb doin' all the time- playin' with their sprinklers?"

"Couldn't find it- twere under half a ton a rubble." shouted Nathan. "You never did 'ev the gentle touch."

"Well, if you buggers dun want a 'and, I'sll piss off 'om!"

"No" shouted Jago. " Just don't go at it like than bull of yourn at some fresh-faced heifers!"

"Tin't their faces 'e d'be interested in.

They were about to get down to some serious work when a voice with a distinct Welsh twang called out:

" I say, who's in charge here? I say, stop that!"

And a little man in green Wellingtons, with what were obviously grey suit trousers tucked in, topped off with a very bright fluorescent orange jacket, yellow vest and a white hard hat scrambled over the rubble.

"You can't do that . You've not got your hi-vizes on for start. Nor your hard hats. Who's in charge?" And he looked round the sweating faces.

"I know you. " he said, pointing at Hezekiah.

"Oh, yeah-? And who the fuck are you?" H tended to get quite Anglo-Saxon when aggravated.
"I'm the Council!"
"Any one in particular?"asked Jago.
"I'm Cornwall, of course. And you can't start work without the right authority. And some barrier tape."
"You can see we already# got a fuckin' barrier- Half the fuckin' 'ill," said Steve.
"I should be most grateful if you weren't all so offensive. Some of us do not approve of language!"
"What d'you want instead? Gesture?" And Hezekiah gave him the finger.
"We'm only trying to get on, help usselves, before your lot can get 'ere. Surely speed is of the essence?" Jago was trying a little placatory logic.
"But we don't know! There may be people buried under there- just think of that poor woman in Looe!"
" There in't no bugger under there. Us d'ev knowd by now,"said H. "What we'm tryin' to do is get the fuckin' road open, so as the fuckin' beer lorry can get through!"
"How like you lot!"

"Never 'eard of sarcasm, sunshine? An' of course, none o' you Welsh 'as ever taken a drop in yer lives!. Not that you could call that Brains stuff 'beer'- not proper. You'd drown before you got pissed."

CHAPTER 3

"More tea, Vicar?"

Up at the White House, they were unaware of the antagonism caused by the arrival of the authorities. They had both agreed that at least one of the builders should be invited to join the committee and Lady Olivia had suggested Jago.

"I'm sure they're all very capable but I do find Hezekiah's language so irksome. I'm sure he's totally unaware of giving offence -it's natural to him, like breaking wind but when you think that I used to be sent to the nursery with no tea for saying 'bother', you may get some idea."

"Oh, I do so agree."said the Vicar. "Do you think we should consider the parable of the talents- get those in the village with special gifts to use them to help us?."

"Those who live here or that growing hoard of 'second-home owners' ? From what Dorothy tells me, some of them are so wealthy that they are buying these million-pound monstrosities with their annual bonuses! What a pity the Good Lord could not have directed his deluge on their new foundations, rather than those of the Church Hall? I'm

sorry, not very Christian of me but certainly heart-felt!"
Several large, modern very expensive houses had recently been squeezed into the one piece of open ground left in the village. Most people had believed that its inaccessibility would prove its defence but the villagers were innocent of the caprices of the County Planners and the real power of money: it not only talked loud but also shifted earth and dug deep.

" You're not thinking of simply toddling up to their front door and asking them to fund the entire thing? Where is our 'esprit de corps', our community spirit?"

"Well, if takings at the last jumble sale are anything to go by, our community spirit is at its lowest I've ever seen. How much did we take, Jerry?"

Jeremy tapped briefly on his miracle tablet.

"Seventy four pounds, forty nine pee. And several centimes, or whatever the hundredth of a euro is called these days."

"But we used to make hundreds of pounds. Hundreds! And that was a few years back. Where is our communal generosity?"

"Along with many of that community- gone up in smoke or else buried in the church yard. I have had a considerable crop recently- although I don't think 'crop' is the right word. We shan't be expecting a crop. At least, not until the Final Coming. "

There was a moment's reflection.

"I already said my John could be of some use." They had forgotten Dorothy

,"And I'm sure he will be, dear, eventually. "

"In a practical way, Dorothy. And, I hope you don"t mind me asking, Lady Olivia, but talking of practicalities, do you think we could have another cup of coffee?"

"Of course,dear- how remiss of me. Dorothy?" So Dorothy had to heave her fifteen-stone into the kitchen, away from the hub of activity.

"I do think it would be right to ask some of the second-homers. Politically, at least," said her Ladyship.

"I agree," said the Vicar," But which? They're all for the most part 'yachties' and all have rather similar interests, namely their yachts. As long as they can drive their 4 by 4s as near to their cottages as possible,-"

fastidious eater and now that age had reduced her appetite even further, she was more than fashionably thin.

"Do we know if he's still here? Jeremy, would you give 'the Crow's Nest' a tinkle? Or whatever inappropriate tune their 'phone plays these days."

Not only the Admiral 'in' but at least a couple of his sons and several grandchildren were still 'down' and the Vicar invited himself and Lady Olivia over for a glass of sherry, to discuss "campaign strategy" before Lunch.

"And then of course, there's always Michael." The enigma behind the Tudor brick wall of the Garden House.

"Do you think we should?"

"He might feel left out if we don't."

"One at a time." said Lady Olivia. She mounted her mobility scooter, of which there was a flotilla in the village, and headed off while the Vicar trotted along beside her.

Jeremy went back to the Vicarage to start on the minutes.

Discussions were getting nowhere at the foot of the hill when, an hour or so later, the unmistakable sound of a police-car, blues and twos going, could be heard on the outskirts of the village. It screeched to a halt as an elderly lady stepped out into the road and beat the bonnet with her cane..

"Don't you know that this is a restricted zone?!" she had asked of the harassed driver as he lowered his window. "Twenty miles an hour! The signs are obvious enough And we had a right old hoo-ha getting the council to agree to it. Had to go to a bloody silly committee meeting in Truro. Do you know how long it takes for us who don't drive any more to get to Truro?! We won't have the authorities breaking the limit!"

"But this is an emergency!" said PC Drake.

"One of these days" said old Mrs Thomas, for it was she, one of the brigade of little white haired old ladies, virtually indistinguishable, who daily patrolled the village, partly to maintain the status quo and partly for exercise. "One of these day there'll be a real emergency-then you'll be sorry. And don't think I haven't taken your number because I have!"

It was one of the many troubles brought on by being based so far away from these unheard-of out of the way little places on the coast; the Police 'Hub'- the latest name for the Cop-shop- which was where they were based in Bodmin, was still nearly 20 miles away and unless the criminals were thoughtful enough to commit their crime during office hours, weekdays only, when the office in Looe was manned and CCTV cameras turned on,, it was those based in Bodmin who had to respond.. Raymond Chandler had his heroes go down 'mean streets' in those books that had so encouraged Drake as a boy to go into Law and Order. Out here, though. it was winding, muddy, narrow, inescapable lanes with great high Cornish banks on either side and tractors in front you had to go down. You couldn't have gone any quicker had you wanted to, it wasn't possible to do that trip safely in less than half an hour, blues and twos and all.

And for the last half hour, PC Drake had been talked at by Inspector Ronald Foot. It had long been Inspector Foot's ambition to be promoted to the Met and be known as 'Foot of the Yard', but, to date, there was little sign of this happening.

"Of course, when you understand the criminal mind as I

do, you will find that every offence will be a display of psychotic behaviour." Foot had had to read up on psychosis as part of his exams and now he used every opportunity to display the dubious nature of this newly-gained knowledge. "And once you've got a grasp of that, you've got it cracked."

Foot was of the opinion that just about everybody was against him and his 'comrades-in-arms'-and he did wish more of them were allowed to carry arms; how he had got through the vigorous vetting of the modern police force, no-one was quite sure but it did possibly explain his indefinite secondment to the Devon and Cornwall Police. If they had been able to insist that he was stationed even further west, they would have done, but Bodmin was second best.

"Does that include parking on a double yellow line?" asked Drake.

"What!?"

"Is double parkin' psychotic? Or letting your dog shit an' not pickin' it up? "

Foot thought quickly and the replied: "Of course not. And

that is why we, the Police, no longer bother ourselves with such things. Employ specialist firms to deal with the petty-fogging issues."

"Which means nobody chases up dog-shit."

"What has dog...er-doings got to do with anything? Really, Drake, your thought patterns are remarkable."

"No, but that's just it. Now we'm specialists, these little things tend to get forgot-"

"Gotten,"corrected Foot. "They're not forgotten...it's just that it is now somebody else's job to remember them. Now, tell me something about this place."

"The village? In't much to tell. They don't commit crimes that often, so we don't get called out that often."

"But I thought that this was your...'beat'?"

"But that's half the problem. We don't have 'beats' no more. Can't remember the last time I actually got out the car down 'ere. P'rpas just to have a quick pee on the quay last summer.. Some of the finest lavatories in the Duchy, they has- Trouble is, they can't afford to keep them open."

"You mean, they keep them clean but shut?!"

" That's about it- Wintertimes, yes- that's the way they can keep them so clean."

"There is, I suppose, a certain nice logic about that."

"Trouble is, when you're bustin', you end up goin' round the back and peein' in the corner."

"Which is against the law."

"When needs must..."

"I just hope no-one saw you. Right. Got your boots?"

"I'm wearin' em," was the surprised answer.

"No, not your issue, black leather. You'll have a nightmare cleaning that lot off. First rule of being a good copper, clean boots."

"What lot?

"That!" said Foot, nodding through the windscreen at the stationary river of mud, masonry and whatever other effluent had come out of the Village Hall and which now was gently settling around the police car.

"I wasn't intending to set foot in it, sir."

"Nonsense. We have to experience what our punters are experiencing. "

"But you've only got shoes on?" And very neat Italianate slippers they were, too.

"Ah, but I was a wise virgin!"

"Sir?!" There had been talk at the station but...

"Come prepared, didn't I? In the boot. Fetch them for me, will you, Constable?"

"Sir?"

"My Wellingtons. They're in the boot. Put them there before we left. Pop round and get them for me, there's a good fellow."

"But, sir-"

"There are ranks, you know, Constable and I, as an Inspector, am considerably senior to you. Please do as you're asked. I shouldn't want to get all hoity-toity."

"But you already are-"

"Constable!"

Drake tried to tiptoe- in so far as it was possible to tiptoe in size twelves- through ankle-deep muck and fetched the Inspector's rather smart blue and white rubber boots.

" I didn't know you sailed, sir?"

"I don't!"snapped Foot,"But you never know, some day. Now. Who's in charge here?"

The Admiral and Lady Olivia totalled nearly one hundred and eighty years between them and they had known each other for more than sixty of them. Installed in an antique love seat in the bay window of 'the Crow's Nest', the two old gentlefolk seemed ignorant of the magnificent views that has first brought them both here;instead, they looked at each other seriously.

"Well, Olive,my dear, I suppose one could simply send for the Marines. That is, if we've got any to spare. What with Arctic training and that little unpleasantness in the Gulf, they're probably all tied up."

"Oh, if I may interrupt here, Admiral."

"Go ahead, Padre. Forgot you was there. Faced with this vision of pulchritude, don't you know."

"Oh, Bobby," blushed Lady Olivia.

"I may be speaking out of turn but I do feel that this catastrophe may be a miracle in disguise. "!

"Always got to put yer spin on it, haven't you? But then, I suppose that is yer job. Go ahead."

So, the Vicar expounded.

"This dreadful nanny state of ours, doesn't matter which lot are in, it does far too much for us. We're far too dependent- this may be a chance for us, the village, indigenous and incomers together, to actually do something together. If your Navy chaps... your 'hearts of oak 'came in with all their gear and rippling torsos, like in those field gun races at Earls Court... helicopters and landing craft and things going off 'bang'- treating this like some outlying Burmese village that had been swamped by the tsunami , well- we'd just stand by and let them and then, once it was done, grumble about how long it took."
"Well, Cornwall won't get it done any quicker?!"
"No, no-sadly not. The Cornish ethos of 'dreckly' has sunk deeply into the mind-set of the Council workers, even those that were not born in the Duchy."
"Osmosis, I think the boffins call it," said the Admiral, "And aren't you being a bit generous when you put 'mind-set' and 'Cornwall Council' together in the same sentence? I had stokers with more nous than most of the Cornwall County Council workers. "
"But we're not here to sling mud,"said Lady Olivia, " Well,

we are in a way. I'm sure there's more than enough still down in the village. What we were really wondering was if you or some of your family might like to join in the adventure?"

"Well, neither you nor I, m'dear, are up to flinging shit-if you'll pardon the expression-We're past it.. Even my boys aren't in exactly the first flush of youth-"

"But the next generation?"suggested the Vicar." Surely you must have at least one of them, at a loss, about the house, due for a gap year or something? Been sent down for some unspeakable jape...?"

"Oh- we've got several around the place- I'm never sure who's here. We'll have a confab at dinner and let you know. Lovely to have seen you, Olive. You really must call more often."

The Vicar escorted Lady Olivia along the cliff, back to the White House and ignoring her invitation to share a sandwich, set off to confront the famous Michael.

Chapter 4

"Well, somebody must be in charge!"

Inspector Foot and PC Drake had appeared over the rubble and Foot's interjection broke the seething silence.

"At last." said the Welshman, "The boys in blue. Better late than never."

"We had to check some other incidents '*en route*'.," said Foot, by way of excuses.

"And stick to the speed limits," said Black.

"And you are?" asked the Inspector, getting on, to disguise their apparent tardiness.

"County," said the little man, cockily.

"Well, Mr County-first time I've heard that name, eh, Drake?" he said, aside.

"No,Prothero. My name's Prothero, I work for the County! Highways."

"So, Mr Prothero, are you responsible for the dreadful state of the roads?" asked Drake." Some of the pot-holes round here could be used to trap elephants.!"

" Rock on," said Steve, the farmer. "First sensible thing I ever 'eard a copper say!"

"That's enough," snapped Foot. "We are not hear to discuss the state of the roads-"

"Cos case you 'adn't noticed, we've not got one here, fer the moment. A road, that is." added Jago.

"I am trying to explain to these..'people'," said Mr Prothero, as if there was something unpleasant in the meaning of the word," that they cannot just come here and start digging! No hard hats, no special clothes, no barrier tape-"

"Just ready to fuckin' graft". 'H' had been quiet for too long.

"Listen-" suggested Jago, "If you go and fetch your dumper an' Steve 'ere were to lend us his tractor- you'm 'ardly ploughin', this weather, are you, mate?"

Steve shook his head," No, but I can stop along o' the tractor an' do the actual diggin'." (Here he raised his voice so that Mr Prothero and the police could hear)," I don't think 'e's insured for any bugger else and we'd 'ate to break regulations."

"But you must have tape!" Prothero was almost in tears. " Officers, you must carry tape, In case of RTAs.?"

" Case of what?" asked Foot,

"Road traffic accidents," said Drake, under his breath, to

try, reluctantly, to help his superior. Then, aloud, "Yes, sir- in the car. "

"Well?!"

"At the top of the hill, sir. Above the landslip."

"I repeat, well? You'll just have to go and get it."

"I'm not exactly dressed for clambering..."

"Hop on, Plod!" It was Steve. "I got to take this old boy." He nodded towards H,"To fetch 'is dumper. You can ride on the back. So, H, where's 'e too?"

Hezekiah knew very well that he had left the truck in its usual spot, half on the pavement , diagonally across double yellow lines, completely obscuring a 'No Parking' sign, so he didn't want to draw too close attention to it, especially with a policeman on the pillion.

" You just drop me off at the top, boy" he said

"Sure?"

"Sure. The walk'll do me good."

Chapter 5

The Vicar had walked out to the headland at the edge of the village. The little lanes out that way were busier than usual as the villagers were finding roundabout ways to get to the quay or wherever they wanted to reach when normally they would have used the hill, so it took him half an hour as he was stopped by each and every one and asked what he thought was going to happen. Two of the more argumentative of the locals asked him if he thought that this was all part of God's larger plan and the Vicar had to plead an urgent errand in order to avoid some very complex doctrinal discussions.

He stopped at the gate in a high, blank wall of old red brick that completely hid the house and garden that lay within as well as the sea beyond.. He wasn't even sure if he ought to be disturbing the occupants as they very much kept themselves to themselves. "And it's hardly surprising," he thought.

Michael Donohue -the Michael Donohoe, lead singer ,guitarist and founder of Michael and All Angels, one of the great rock bands of the 1990s and Noughties actually owned a house in which he lived, on and off, here in the village, behind this wall. Behind this very door!

Which opened!

If he were honest, when relating this later to Jeremy , Trevor would not have expected who it was. The thought of some vast hirsute hulk wearing a tight black tee-shirt bearing the legend 'Security' and swinging a greasy motor-cycle chain nonchalantly in one massive fist would not have surprised him- he had watched the Altamont video. Or a smooth record executive in a suit- no-one wore suits in the village, except for their all-purpose BDMs- (births, deaths and marriages) . Or even a sexy groupie. But he had not expected what looked like a three foot high Ewok escaped from a Star Wars film.

"Hullo. I'm Jake." said the Ewok. "Please come with me." And he held out his hand and led the Vicar, shuffling through the winter garden towards the back door where stood what would have been an unassuming figure were it not for the fact that it was wrapped in what appeared to be Chewbacca's hide.

"Hello, I'm Michael. This is Jake."

The Ewok answered: "I've already told him."

"Well, then, I'm sorry to have wasted my breath. We know who you are."

"You're the Vicar. God's representative on Earth." said the little creature." What's He like?"

"Well, I-I-I.."

"My mother is living with Him now."

"Let's get him indoors before we start giving the Vicar the third degree. shall we? " He opened wide the door which lead into one of those kitchens that looked like a TV set. It only needed Nigella to be flowing across its stainless steel work tops or Jim thrust into the wood-fired pizza oven in the corner for things to become really unreal.

"We all love to cook." Michael explained, as he stepped out of the costume. Jake, too, was emerging from his selection of furs and sacking.

"I got them after the wrap-party. Neat, eh? Certainly keep you warm."

"If you play out in the garden in those for too long, there'll be sightings. Coast guards, life boat and possibly even the police." said the Vicar.

"Oh," said Michael, stroking his son's hair, cut fashionably shaggy. "I hadn't thought."

"No sign of Estuary English when he speaks", thought the Vicar. "Definite plus. He's never fifty!"

"What are the first two?" asked Jake.

"First two what, babe?"

"You said we're going to give him the third degree- what are...?"

"The First Two. I see. Well, tell you what...go find Mrs. G and ask her to help you to Google it while I talk to our guest."

" You mean you don't know!"

"Exactly!. Ah, Mrs. G," and a lady appeared from within the house, her grey hair up in a bun; a homely soul, could be sixty, dressed in oaten coloured sensible clothes, textured tights and even more sensible shoes.

" This is Mrs, G- Mrs. Guthrie. She has been my rod and my staff- well, certainly my staff, ever since Joanna died."

" That 's my mother. She's gone to be with Jesus."

"Oh, I'm sorry-" The Vicar was rather fazed by such candour.

"Oh, we're not sorry or sad any more,"said the boy, "Leastways, not often- though I did miss her a lot at Christmas, even though we were at Granny and Grandpa's."

"I'm sure the Vicar didn't come to hear our stories- we haven't let him get a word in edgeways-" And the father and son completed the well-polished routine together- "Like fish-slice.!" Jake giggled irrepressibly as his father first ticked him, then kissed him and then slapped his bottom lightly, propelling him towards his house-keeper. "He wants to know the origin of the term- 'third degree'. Not 'murder'- but 'giving the third degree- you know. He can use the Mac but don't let him go looking for things he shouldn't." The little boy ran on ahead and the lady followed

"Can I get you coffee? I'm going to make some," And he turned on the Tassimo. "Makes a wicked Mocha which the boy loves."

"He seems a lovely child."

"He is and I'm going to make damn sure he stays that way."

He stood in silence, looking at the space where the boy had been, then turned." Now, what can I do for you?"

"I don't want to stop now but it's about the landslide- it took the Church Hall with it-"
"No way!?"
"I thought you'd have known?- all those helicopters. They were press."
"Oh. I thought it was one of our rather ostentatious friends dropping in after a late night in London. Or anywhere! I'm sure all your parishioners think it's me."
"Oh..." The Vicar found it difficult to deny. Michael was an obvious target and yes, on several occasions, he and his guests had arrived by helicopter . But not recently.
"Oh, my God! Oh, sorry ,Vicar but I haven't looked at the news, or anything-emails, Twitter, nothing- that's the joy of being here. But you were saying..?"And he got up ,crossed to a kitchen drawer and took out a large chequebook. The Vicar noticed by the way that it was issued by Coutts Bank before he realised:
"Oh, no- no- we're not asking for money. Well, not yet.. I was wondering..well, Lady Olivia and I- have you met Lady Olivia? The White House?"
"Oh, wow! So there really is someone still living there? I

thought it was another legend. No but I'd really love to-"
"That's rather what she said about you-We were wondering, if you be prepared to be our President ?
Of the Committee. The Reconstruction Committee. We haven't thought of a snappier name yet- It's your name as much as anything but if you'd actually mange to come to some meetings..and take part..?."
"But of course, I'd love to- I'm honoured . When do we start? "

The village, whilst possessing only the one road wide enough for cars to pass, -Fore Street , for the time being, completely blocked-, was in fact a maze of paths and inclines, slopes and steps , easily accessible to the erstwhile donkeys which helped to build the place but which sadly were no more. A very aged one was kept as a sort of pet but no longer as a logistics solution for access which was very difficult for cars

Arguments at the bottom of the landslide had moved slowly up the hill and the re-builders and Mr Prothero were discussing was appeared to be a growing problem, the continuing flow of water- not much but still a disturbing dribble, from beneath the rubble.

"You said you turned off the water?"

"Yes, my mother's livid."

"So this isn't coming from the mains?"

"No."

"So?"

"Could be a spring we didn't know?"

"But why is it surfacing only now?"

They looked at each other and then at the newly-built ranch-style house that had been squeezed into a fragment of land above where the Hall had been.

"Oh, no!" said Mr Prothero,under his breath to himself, "Not again!"

Detective Inspector Foot chose to take this opportunity to 'get to know the territ'ry', as he put it to PC Drake. "Got to know yer territ'ry, First rule of being a good copper."

"I thought clean boots was the-?"

"Get a feel of the place. Is there any way I can walk back up to the car? Must be a path or something?"

"No problem, sir. You follow the signs to the coast path, that'll get you up to the cliff and you'll remember where I left the car?"

"Of course. I have a nose for direction. I was renowned for it in basic training. Called me the Bloodhound!" What Foot didn't know was that the instructors were referring to his looks rather than his sense of direction .

"In that case, sir, do you mind if I pop in and see my Auntie Cissie? She's 84, has lived here most of her married life- Uncle Jack come from here- he's dead, of course and she'll be completely lost with the phones down."

"Of course. Don't let it be said that I'm a slave-driver. Is half an hour enough? "

"It'll give me an excuse to get away."

"Right. Do we need to synchronize watches?"

"I make it just after 10."

"Ten-oh-three it is. Make it so" And he pressed one of the several knobs on his very obvious wristwatch.

"Divers'", he said, nonchalantly as he saw the constable looking at it.

"Pardon?"

"Divers' watch. It's what they all wear. Well, what we all wear."

"I didn't know...?"

"Oh, yes-there's a scuba school in the Leisure Centre, Monday evenings. I've even got the knife you strap on to your leg."

"Not much call for that in the Leisure Centre?"

"It's all about equilibrium-got to get your weight and balance right so you need all the gear."

"Just hope the classes doesn't clash with duty roster."

"I've already sorted that with the Sergeant. No, no- you go and find your auntie, I'll just....nose about."

"That famous bloodhound nose again,eh, sir?"

"What? Eh? Oh, yes- yes. "And he tapped it and set off, following it.

He got thoroughly lost after the first few alleyways but one thing he did notice. There was smoke in the air. It was a smell he was sure he recognised. He sniffed. Strong smoke. Almost all the cottages that had anyone in them had smoke coming from the chimneys. But this is a smokeless zone, he thought, surely. Something to check on.

"You noticed it too, eh?" A voice interrupted his cogitation.

"What?"

" I thought you would. I've been watching you," Foot looked at the speaker.

Although he might have been well over six foot at full stretch, the figure who looked back at him over one shoulder was cringing in what appeared to be a perpetual grovel, his natural pose, as if ready to block and parry anything that the world would-and did- throw at him.

He was an unusual sight in Porthwallow, even though he appeared to live there, obviously not a working man nor really dressed like a yachtie nor a retired man of leisure..

He wore a leather cap of the sort worn by Marlon Brando in' A Street Car named Desire", but several sizes too small. His rheumy eyes- the traditional 'lightly-poached eggs' were accentuated by small rimless glasses while his chin had given up the struggle of supporting his bulbous bottom lip and taken refuge some where around his Adam's apple. But all this was diminished by the nose and the growth beneath. Think of a large bulb of smoked garlic and you're half way towards the nose but what can only be described as the moustache, because of its position *vis a vis* the nose upon the face, evoked a small exploded iron-wool tutu, some of which had taken refuge below his mouth into what really did not deserve the name of 'goatee'. Inevitably, when he did remove the cap, he revealed that he was a devotee to the comb-over, a style to become even more popular because of the latest American president.. The few strands that had survived beneath the cap across his head were grey. He wore a full-length leather coat in an attempt to appear artistic, maroon cords and yellow desert boots.

"I do that, you know. Watch people, that is. For my work. I see you were with a member of the uniformed branch so presume you are too are Police? You don't mind me interrupting your train of thought. In case you need...ah.. some...ah.. untainted information, shall we say? These locals are terrible liars. Put it out that I was a spy! Huh, what could you spy on down here? OK, there <u>are</u> several ground-floor bathrooms, put in by all these newcomers, with windows which are sometimes left open on a warm evening but really..to suggest that I actually might peep...The case was dismissed through lack of evidence.. My card." And he handed the Inspector an embossed card with the words: 'Cyril Oliphant. Writer.' on it.

"Thank you. Most helpful. And what do, or did you write, Mr Oliphant?"

If he could have cringed even further then he would as he replied: "Less said, sooner mended. eh, K.W.I.M? But shall we just say I've been vetted by GCHQ?!" And he crept off.

"Drake," Foot asked the constable, once he had found the car and his colleague. " What does-um K.W.I.M. mean? Is this one of these kid's things, like LOL, or SWALK, like we had when we were young -well, some people- not me but....?"

"'Know What I Mean,' I think, sir. It's off one of those telly shows."

"That explains it."said Foot, and then he remembered his other observations.

"Aren't we in a smokeless zone here?"

"But they've had coal fires here ever since the ships was steam-driven. Probably before. A few bags used to disappear regular. Taken as perks o' the job, for the lads as worked at the docks and then it was spread where needed round the village. 'Course, the incomers, second-homers, they all 'as 'ad wood burners put in, one of the first things they do, but the indigenous, they swears by coal- and proper coal, not they nuggets. My gran kept her coal in the bath. Fires lit with copies of the Daily Mirror, n'all- not fire lighters!"

As much as could be done had been done, given the time of year and other calls upon the County emergency road crews and, as long as it didn't bucket down again, they thought they'd be safe.

Unfortunately, there had been another minor slip on the North coast but it had been right next door to a new, adults-only boutique hotel and spa that was very expensive and very popular with editors of national newspapers, retired Cabinet ministers and the like, which meant that what interest there was in the situation in Cornwall was concentrated there, especially as there was a crack in the drive to one of the luxury suites.

So, that evening, Jago Hocking headed for the meeting at the White House and could hardly believe his eyes as he saw one of his all-time heroes, Michael Donohoe heading in the same direction, not as a character from 'Star Wars' but as himself.

"Hi, I'm Michael" he called.

"Yes," replied Jago, " I know," and then kicked himself for sounding like your archetypal village idiot.." Sorry, no- Jago. I'm Jago."

"I've heard about you- and only good things!" said Michael with a laugh, in which Jago joined with pride.

The first thing Michael did was to graciously accept the honour of the Presidency of the Church Hall Reconstruction Committee, Vice-presidents, Lady Olivia Vincent and Admiral of the Fleet Sir Robert Hawkins (retired). Those present: Jago Hocking:

"I'm makin' sure the voice of the Indigenous is heard," he said when he was introduced to the committee," Never get none o' we on any of they other committees- WI an' that..."

"But you in't a woman, you daft tit," replied Jenny Thomas, who spoke as she found. She explained that she was mainly representing the Players as they were one of the few groups that actually used the Hall but those that knew her were aware that they wouldn't have been able to keep her away from this gathering, even if they had tried.

"They say they'm sending someone from the W.I. but they'm that short of members, the only two who is still under 70, the Praed sisters, is fightin' over who it's gonna be and as for Age Concern, neither o' they thought they couldn't ,in all honesty, do much, specially after dark."

Henry Lake from the shop was there and offered to act as Treasurer: 'until we can find a proper accountant who won't charge' ;then there as the Vicar and of course Jeremy Timmins, adopted '*nem con*' as Secretary; Alexandra Sutton from the school ,a pretty woman in her early thirties, Bobby Hawkins, early twenties and something of a hunk which, fortunately, he was unaware of, the one of the Admiral's grandchildren who happened to be 'down' and Alf, age indeterminate , the milkman, who said he was representing the Regatta committee, and anyway knew everybody in the

village as he delivered milk to. When Alf was introduced, Michael asked him if he did soya and if so, could they have a word after, about deliveries.
"Now before we elect a Chair-"said Lady Olivia.
"Honestly, Olive- can't we do without all that political correctness stuff?" asked the Admiral." A chair is a chair - dumb and static, usually made of wood, until it has a bum sitting on it. Can I suggest we have a chairman, a chair woman or even, Heaven help us- no, no, Vicar, I wasn't calling on you -a chair person if you insist! But not some bloody Chippendale!." And then after a moment's thought." Unless it's one of those bodybuilder chappies but I imagine the Full Monty would be too distracting at meetings like these. Play havoc with the digestion."
"Yes, dear-"said Lady Olivia, used to placating old men ", but before we do anything like that- I'm sorry to say, I have had a telegram," And she held up the piece of paper in question. (8669)
"A telegram? !" exclaimed Jenny, echoing Edith Evans' intonation from 'The Importance.'
"From dear Letitia."

The faces of those in the know fell while Michael simply echoed the name.

"Letitia'.? I don't think I've met...."

"Mrs Butt, sir.?" Even the Admiral seemed in awe. "Letitia Butt. You must have heard the name?!No? You obviously very wisely keep yourself to yourself."

"Not been -er-'summoned'?" asked Jago.

He was trying not to ogle Michael. Having one of Rock and Roll's Hall of Fame at the same table as him was taking some getting used to. He explained:

"'er 'usband bought old Mrs. Langmaid's place on Fore Street there- an' when I say 'old' Mrs Langmaid, I'd mean Daphne's mother-in-law, Jangle's gran.- backalong- in the 50's. Father says 'E was something in the Government,- Mr Butt, that is, not my father- then, but that was when being something in the Government was worth bein' proud of, not somethin' you got to apologise for, resign and then line yer pockets with from the resultin' directorships. They used to give their whole lives- not resign at 60 with a guaranteed knight'ood .Oh, sorry, Admiral," he said, in response to the Admiral's unsurprising 'herrumpf'. " But don't start me on

that- ."
There was a pause but Jago couldn't let it lie.

."'Ow can one man 'ave two jobs or more, directorships, each paid more in a year 'n I s'll ever earn in my entire life..? No. I said I shan't." He took deep breath." Anyways.. They come 'ere backalong because they liked it, not because everybody else in their Party, including the Prime Minister was comin' 'ere for one of their many annual 'olidays, stroke photo opportunities like they does today. I can remember 'im, the old man, just. Wore they baggy khaki shorts. They was 'is one concession towards being on 'oliday. Always carried a rolled umbrella. An' a filthy sun-'at which they do say 'e wore at El Alamein. Along with the umbrella. And the shorts. Father said 'e was a good old boy-""

Lady Olivia had to stop him, "Jago, dear- I'm sure we're all absolutely captivated but we're rather off the point. Fate of so many committees. Anyway, it seems Letitia's coming by tomorrow's train, insists nothing is done without her and expects to be collected from Bodmin. I was wondering, Jeremy, dear- if you might...?"

"Do you know which train?"

"The ten o'clock from Paddington- bound to be." It was the one the Admiral used, so he presumed that the rest of the world did too..

Jeremy agreed.

"Excuse me-" It was the first time that Michael had interrupted.

"Yes, er- Mr...?"

"Oh, no- please call me 'Michael'. But , I know I'm an incomer- and a newish one at that, but surely this is an emergency. I don't see how we can waste time,waiting for anyone. Even if it were the Second Coming. Sorry, Vicar. Can I, in the absence of a chairman, assert my role as President and recommend we... get on with things?!"

"Delightful,"

"How refreshing!"

"Right on, bro!"

Chapter 6

"Bloody good bloke."

That was the committee's general opinion of Michael , although he, ("Must check on Jake") along with Lady Olivia ("Too much excitement in one day")and the Admiral,"Way past my bed time") the Vicar and Jeremy ("A sermon to re-write"), and Alexandra ("Preparation. And marking." "Tis simple", Jago had replied,"Don't give 'em so much o' the one and 'ee won' 'eve so much to do of t' other.") and Alf who always had a five o'clock start, had refused the offer of a pint down the C*ourt*. Bobby had asked if he could come along and Jenny immediately had him in a mock half-Nelson..

"'Course you can! A new man in the village. We 'll all be after' ee!"

Though seemingly said in jest, Bobby was soon to discover just how true this was to be.

"Well,"asked Tegan, "Where is he? I thought I was going to meet a superstar at last." She was on duty again that evening.

"Gone home to check on his boy. And that's not what I expected, either."

"Bloody good bloke."
"So, set the world to right, have you?" asked Tegan.
"No. Quite sensibly he sent us all of home to think. Not waste time witterin' in committee, not this time, but all go and come back, two days time, with ideas."
"That must 'ev fuckin' annoyed you, maid." 'H' had been the only customer in the place when they had come in and he was only there to pick up the latest news; he enjoyed a bantering relationship with Jenny.
"What!?"
"Bein' told to fuckin' shut up an' think before you opens your mouth fer once!"
" That's the last time I opens me mouth for you, then, Hezekiah Pemberthy- or if'n I do, I 'sll bite it off.!"
"Jenny! Please, this isn't the place." Charlie and Doris had come down to the bar when they had heard the door. " I don't want to ban you cos we need every penny we can get, but keep it clean. You'll frighten off this young man, for a start."
Bobby smiled and then laughed nervously. "Oh, don't mind me."

"Well, if he's a chip off the old block, he'll do fine. This is one of the Admiral's grandsons," she explained.
"Oh," said Doris, bustling forward in the presence of a male under forty, "And what do we call you, then?"
"Well, I'm Robert, too- named after Gramps- but they call me 'Bobby' , to avoid complications."
"And do you have any.... thespian inclinations?" asked Jenny, as Jago put a pint in front of him.
*Oh, give the boy a chance."said Tegan, "Hasn't even had a chance to have a sip of his beer and you're signing him up! " She launched her dazzler at Bobby, who blushed again.
"All right," said Jenny and looked Tegan fully in the face."But I saw him first."

Jenny Thomas was the power behind, and the glory of the Porthwallow Players, as she was of just about everything she involved herself with. Born in the village in the late 1960s, she had followed a number of her friends to the local sixth-form college- "it'll be a good laugh."- and thoroughly misbehaved in all of the classes that she turned up for, with the notable exception of hair-dressing, mainly because it was 'hand's on' and there wasn't a back row in which she could slump and insult the teachers, which had been her primary pursuit in other subjects. She came out with a qualification in hair-dressing and beauty and looked around, waiting for Life to begin and while she waited, played around both on her friends and herself, with the more outrageous hair-dos that the big stars wore so that when they hit the Boscarne, the local dance hall in near-by Looe of a Friday, it looked like every night was Walpurgisnacht. Their more remarkable bouffants set her imagination racing. Opposite a washed and wiped face in the mirror, she began to fantasize about who that face might be or might become on the inside as well as the outside and a chance encounter in the Ladies at the Boscarne led to an introduction to a local am-dram group, after which there was no looking back. She had found her element. True, she would often still end Friday nights on her back in one of the beach huts with blokes whose liberal use of Brut could not disguise the fact that they had been fishing all week but she had found something to fill her days and more and more of her nights.

About thirty years or more previous to these events, remarkably and unbeknownst amongst themselves, the village had become the haven for a dozen or so exceptional people, most of them lucky enough to have been able to take early retirement from whatever they had done before and buy some of the nicer houses. It was true that they, like most Brits abroad, had tended to look inward rather than out, to socialize together, rather than make any real effort to integrate with the locals; they tended to gather for gin about seven before dinner rather than follow the local practice of expecting their tea on the table when they got back from work at five before then going out to the pub; they were mostly C of E which had delighted the then incumbent who was beginning to notice the dropping off of congregations that was to become a torrent, the bane of the Reverend Uphill who was now burying most of them. And, one Christmas, after a particularly hilarious game of Charades in one of the larger homes, they had discovered in at least one member of each married couple, a passion for Amateur Dramatics. And after an unexpectedly successful

'*Good Old Days*' when party pieces were aired in the Church Hall, the Porthwallow Players had been born.

They built a stage in the Church Hall (essentially trestles which had to be moved for any clashing event) , they tended to call the Hall 'the Theatre' or even 'the space' by the better informed,

the store room at the side was their Green Room and gradually the lighting was improved from the original footlights- cobbled together from empty Nescafe tins with holes in the bottom for the fitting and the wires) and 'spots' rescued from skips outside other theatres upcountry to something verging on the respectable and most definitely enlightening.

They were incredibly lucky in the make-up of their company- for 'company' it had most definitely become, because not only did at least one man possess the skills for lighting, while another had the expertise for building sets, surpassing many a professional construction in that the doors opened and closed on cue and stayed that way for as long as was necessary while the walls of the sets did not waver at all, but also there were a few of the men who did not take much persuading to tread those boards that they themselves had erected.

Into this magic circle, Jenny had entered. As a still young juvenile lead, she was a God-send and played opposite a number of the husbands. The fact that she also played about with a number of the husbands was, for the most part, ignored. After all, it had been the Eighties, the summer of Love long gone but not forgotten and some of those earlier parties had ended with the car-keys in a bowl on the coffee table when it was simply a matter of trying to avoid the owner of the bicycle clips.

Jenny had been married briefly to one of those beach encounters but he was off the Scottish boats and as the fish diminished down south so did the amount of time he stayed in these waters. Last she had heard of him, he was living in Buckie and working off-shore on the oil rigs. But a bi-product of their transient marriage had been Jim, a fine lad, nearly thirty now, who had joined the Navy as soon as he had been able. The Admiral had lent a hand here; he had had his eye on the boy ever since there had been the slight chance that the child might be the fruit of a visit by one of the Admiral's sons, a hedge-fund manager from New York whose vacation had coincided with the fishing fleet being at sea. His expensive champagne had had the desired effect upon Jenny and he marked it down as both much cheaper and more enjoyable that any escort on Fifth Avenue. A discreet DNA test after the boy was born had proved the Hawkins fears ungrounded but presents would arrive irregularly via the Admiral for Jenny. She prided herself on having brought the child up alone, albeit in the tight community of Porthwallow where every other man was his 'uncle' and every woman his 'auntie', some even related by blood. She was currently married to a long-distance lorry driver which made things comparatively straight-forward. She still went dancing at the Boscarne now and then but had never again ended the night on the beach.

Back home at the Vicarage, Trevor and Jeremy faced each other from their respective arm chairs beside a comfy log fire. One with his Ovaltine, the other his cocoa, the one reinforced with black rum, the other with Tia Maria as was their slightly wicked wont, they reflected on a frantic day and the enormity of the task ahead of them .

"However," said the Vicar, "We know He moves in a mysterious way- "

"Like a crab, I always think that means,"interrupted Jeremy.

"Thank you ,dear- you know what I mean , but I do feel that this might just be what the village not only needs but will come to want."

"The only road in and out completely blocked by a land-side and our Church Hall, the focus of our community in ruins? That mental movement is not even like that of a lobster, let a lone a crab"! 12

"Let me finish. You have to admit, ours is, or has become, a very disparate place. If you think back just to when we came, twenty years ago. For a start, most of the houses were lived in- real homes, not holiday homes, or second homes or whatever you want to call them- lived in, and mostly by, Cornish. Everybody knew everybody else, everybody related to everybody else!- kitchen doors open all day, and many all night- the pub was a pub, not an aspiring bistro, we had shops, twelve shops when we came- bakers, butcher- ok, I admit, no candle-stick maker but then I wonder when anyone actually did have a candle-stick maker- candles, yes- that was what a 'chandlers' was but-"

"You're wandering, Vicar,"Jeremy said with a smile, but behind that smile was the seed of doubt about his partner's mentality..

"Sorry, sorry, but you know what I mean? "

"Absolutely,"

"What I mean is those indigenous who are left are all up in the council houses on the outskirts and there are ghettos of ageing incomers- the Strand, Cliff Road, Channel Heights, places like that, held together by a ..a.. dying coral of holiday homes."

"I say, that's rather good' dying coral""

"I saw that programme about the Great Barrier Reef."

"Oh."

"But it's true but I think this emergency- and Michael, I have to admit it, does look like an absolute Godsend."

"All we need is his army of Archangels and we'll be home and dry."

Chapter 7

First steps

The road was cleared fairly quickly and they had only had to have one emergency supply shipment, which was, truth be told, something of a disappointment for Jago and his cronies. Brought up on the tales of the fleet that had sailed from nearby Fowey to free Europe more than seventy years previous, they had had enormous fun working out the logistics of redirecting all the supplies that would normally have come into the village by road to a nearby landing where they could be loaded into whatever small craft were available and then delivered to the village quay by sea. The most awkward but most devoutly to be wished, were the barrels of beer and the other supplies for the pub; fortunately '*the CoverletArms*' was right on the quay, so the only problem, though a considerable one, was the hefting of the barrels into the boat and subsequently, out again. In the end, despite intricate plans involving tripods, blocks and tackle, ropes, pulleys and yard arms, all worked out by 'H' on the back of an envelop, his favourite design medium, they found that it was easiest simply to lift and chuck. 'H' excused himself on the grounds of an old hernia- "An' if I gets that fucker agen, my missus 'll kill me." but they sent for Steve the farmer who, reunited in his old rugby second-row partnership with Nathan, soon had the barrels off the dray and onto the boat and then reversed the operation onto the quay. The only casualty was a box of Cheesy Wotsits that somehow got mislaid. The one moment of discord was when one of second-homers rang and said that her individual order from the supermarket in St Austell couldn't get through and would they send the boat for it; it was then that Jago felt obliged to limit himself to one of 'H's favourite expletives.

The same abrupt reply was made to this same lady's husband when he complained that his copy of the 'Telegraph' had not been delivered that morning. Apart from that, a line of willing gofers helped to carry what the shop had ordered and it did not go unnoticed that re-victualling the shop by boat and porterage was markedly quicker than the usual chaos when the van simply parked outside and blocked the street for half an hour.

But Life began to return to normal. Tegan had watched the replenishing of the pub and had helped put everything away but she couldn't help focusing on the Admiral's grandson, Bobby. Although he had not yet filled out like the older rugby players, he possessed a fine frame and had shifted more than his share. Here was a boy for whom the old cliche 'with laughing eyes' was really right. Even in the midst of winter, there was a sun-bleached tint to his brown hair- he'd been skiing over the New Year with chums in Meribel ;he hadn't shaved that morning and, with the exertion of the unloading, had removed both his puffa jacket and his lumberjack shirt, leaving only a sweat-stained blue vest She could not help her imagination stirring and actually, albeit unconsciously, she licked her lips. When the unloading was over and he was dressing again, she casually asked him if, as a visitor, he'd like her to show him around.

"Well," he said, laughing, "Of course, I'd love to but really, you know, I've been coming down here to stay with Gramps almost all my life and I expect I've played hide and seek in most of the more obscure corners."

Tegan smiled back and then said slowly: "Oh, I bet there's one or two...'nooks and crannies'... you may have overlooked. I'm off at three and it don't look like rain."

The first place they went to was 'the Castle'. At least, that was what the locals called it but the more prissy academics who came down now and then to poke around out there insisted that it was a 'blockhouse'.

It seems that Henry VIII had been paranoid about being invaded by the Holy Roman Empire, eager to get their own back for having declared himself Head of the Church and Defender of the Faith- it seems that there is a long history of the English walking away from European institutions within which they cannot get their own way- and so had dozens of these small fortifications built all along the south coast. This one had great thick walls pierced by several archer's arrow-slits and some stone steps leading nowhere.

"We used to play all sorts up here," said Bobby, starting up one of the now-blind flights.

"Did you never invite any of us locals?" Tegan asked, almost serious.

"You know, I don't think it ever even crossed our minds.

You lot seemed to spend all summer together leaping off the quay, right by the sign that says 'No diving', and we almost always went out in the boats. See, I've got dozens of cousins- we were very ..."

"Snooty?"

"No, I don't think we were, honestly but very close. We still are."

"Bet you didn't play in the Pig Sty."

"But isn't that where the Man who lives in the Woods... goes?"

"When you say-'goes'...?" She left an open-ended question.

"We were always told it was where he went to...er.."

"Shit?"

"Absolutely."

"Where did you get that idea? Why on earth should he stomp all the way up here when he's got thousands of perfectly good trees he can..." And she chose her words precisely,"Defecate beneath"

"Well," said Bobby, rather embarrassed. "I think it started when somebody found a..a turd in there."

"But the sheep shelter there."

"This was definitely human. And warm. And I supposed we all added a real turd to our imagined bogey-man and ..."

"That's how myths begin,"said Tegan, "And pogroms. And anyway, the Man who Lives in the Woods, he isn't a bogey-man- he's real. Some sort of relative of mine- getting on now, though- come on. "

And they made their way up to the cliff top, not really an ideal site for a pig sty but an obvious choice for an observation post.

Chapter 8

For this is what it had been, a far less magnificent and less effective edifice than the Castle, for while the Castle had proved pretty efficient at keeping opposition at bay for hundreds of years, the one enemy plane in 1940 that those inside did spot throughout the War had obviously been flown by a windy crew, for no sooner had they crossed the coast and seen the blacked-out glow of Plymouth, some thirty miles away, than they dumped their bombs willy-nilly and as one of the witnesses had said at the time : "Then the Focker fucked off out of here."

They managed to kill a sheep and traumatise dozens more and every spring at ploughing time for years to come, farmers kept on digging up bits of green-painted bomb casing but fortunately no-one was hurt. The Home Guard corporal, Iggy Holmes, used to tell the story for the price of several pints of rough cider.

"We see'd 'ee, see, and us was arguing as to whether this was the right opportune time to use our one bullet- us had several rifles but only the one bullet. see?, rations- but by the time us 'ed made up our minds, the bugger was 'ere, there, dropped the lot and gone. All us could was duck. Mind you, what Fritz was thinkin' of, bombin' a pigsty, I can't imagine- less'n it was all part a' 'itler's grand plan, tryin' to starve us out, gradual-like. Pigsty by pigsty I mean, rations was short, but a coupla pigs weren't gonna make all that diff'rence to the War Effort. Not in the long run"-

The few of them in the Porthwallow branch of the Home Guard, the old, the halt, the simple and the young, all those that weren't in the air, on or under the sea or fighting a rear-guard in Belgium were quite cosy, and they made the Pig-sty even more so, with the addition of a few home comforts. Over the years, what had been left on VE day had gradually disappeared, stolen or consciously been returned from whence they came but the rudimentary bunk that they had lovingly constructed in the back stall to ease those black nights on duty was still there as well Tegan knew.

"Come on," she said as she ducked into the shed. Bobby was a little slow in following her and was astonished to discover her in the act of removing her T-shirt, revealing no sign of unnatural support.

"Golly!"

"Listen, you've been gazing at them ever since we met, so I thought....why not?"
And backing him up gently against the wall, adroitly removed his puffa jacket and shirt, almost with one movement. Her adeptness extended to his belt and jeans but came up against matters arising in his boxers.
"Well, hello." she said appreciatively. "Now, no,no-wait a minute-"
"I'm not sure I can," wailed Bobby.
"Were you a boy scout?"
"What? What's that got to do with anything?!"
"Were you?" as she removed her phone from her back pocket of her jeans, before easing them to the floor,
"You're not going to take pictures?!"
"No- I just want to know if you're...prepared?"
"I was in the sea cadets,"
"Well, isn't it a good thing us girl guides have the same motto as the boys. Be prepared!" And she slid from between the phone and its cover, two pristine condoms.
"You never know," she said as she applied herself to the matter at hand.

The first was unsurprisingly rather frantic. But the second, phenomenal!

Bobby had hoped for a third but Tegan hadn't come equipped and anyway, had to go to work. As she left him in the Pigsty, she said, enigmatically: "Next time, tis your turn."

Meanwhile, Jeremy had dutifully driven over the Bodmin moor to fetch Letitia Butt from the station. Patiently, he had waited for all the travellers to pass through the gate. When there had been no sign of his passenger, he got out of the car which he had illegally parked by the entrance and wandered unassumingly through the gates and on to the platform. There, at the far end was what he took for a porter as the poor woman was not only weighed down with several bags of various sizes and manufacture, most seemingly old, plastic and from various Knightsbridge stores, and dragging a large suitcase on wheels but also trying to push a wheelchair at the same time. In this chair, Jeremy was to discover, was Letitia Butt, overflowing it in all directions, with a tiny dog on her lap..

"I think that's my driver," she called over her shoulder to the lady porter. "He'll help you. Jeremy, isn't it?" she called, peering along the platform."Take Gracey, there's a good fellow. And mind she doesn't defecate all over the shop. Bloody long way from London, specially if you're a doggikins. Can't explain to her she'd got to keep her legs crossed all that way. " And then, lowering her voice so that only half of Bodmin could hear: "Between you and me, I think she peed in First Class. At least she 's got taste." She handed the rat-sized toy terrier, complete with the pink ribbon on its head, to Jeremy who tried to get acquainted with her but only just avoided a very nasty nip on the end of his nose.

"I should have warned you. She doesn't like men. But I'd have thought, in your case...Still, is that your car?"

Between them, the reluctant lady porter who was in fact the nearest that BR has to a station master and Jeremy managed to get Letitia out of the wheel chair and into the car. Jeremy had not at first noticed the pair of aluminium crutches hidden beneath the the abundance of bags and she had insisted on being installed in the crutches before leaving the chair and attempting the car seat. As this meant covering a distance of less than a yard in which she could hardly turn her vast rump from the one mode of transport to the other , it caused considerable confusion and cries of pain. At hearing her mistress's distress, Mou-mou went on the offensive, barking with a particularly high-pitched yelp and nipping wherever it saw human flesh.

"Isn't she loyal?" said Letitia, once she lay panting in the passenger's seat which had been extended as far as possible to accommodate her. "Understands everything I say. Don't you , darling? Kissy, kissy?" And the little beast started licking her mistress's lips.

On the road from Bodmin to Porthwallow, Letitia hardly drew breath, pontificating on the state of the A38: "Of course, there were no motorways then. Used to chuck all the kids into the Lagonda, sent the staff on down with the luggage by train, spend the first few days stuck on the Exeter by-pass," then on to the church architecture of Cornwall: "Dear Johnny Betjeman, loved him to bits but he was quite wrong about all those one-off saints- they all got off the missionary cobs, made it up the beaches, only to be beheaded there on the sand by Twdrig and his Cornish anthropophagii, -oh, yes, the Cornish celts were definite head-hunters- I'm told some of them still are in the darker corners of the local rugby fields-Hell-fire Corner- oh, yes- Anyway, these milksop missionaries were immediately immortalised as saints in some gem of a church which they didn't deserve- you'll have notice, no doubt, how many are built in the old pagan places, near woodland and running water? Definite signs of druids- just think of our lovely St. Wallow's- holy well and all."

As they neared the village, her scattered brain focused on the matter at hand, as she saw it.

"I shall hold a meeting tomorrow-after eleven as I'm never very good first thing in the morning. I imagine everyone will come to me?"

"Well," said Jeremy, dreading the counter blast," Things are really rather under way, up at Lady Olivia's ."

"Without me?! Unthinkable. How pretentious!"

" I'm sure you'd be welcome..."

"How on earth do they think I can get up there!? Selfish, too.!"

That evening, the Disaster Committee met again around the dining table at the White House. Michael, while still President, had stepped aside as Chairman following the offer of help from Ashley Pine.

" Now, I know you all think I'm a bit of a prat, what with the big motor and bloody expensive 'ouse, but one thing I do know is Committees. I were boss of a firm up-coutry- sold it fer an eight-figure number and that's eight before the decimal point including six noughts! I 'ave chaired more board meetings- both spellings,!- than I like to remember so, I'm not offering tons o' cash- I earned my pile the 'ard way and I'm keepin' it but I will keep this committee on its toes, if that's what you want.!"

"Proposed!" shouted the Admiral.

"Seconded," from the Vicar

"Show of 'ands?" asked Ashley and every hand shot up.

"Right. Passed 'nem con. Thank you, and I'd like my thanks minuted, Mr. Secretary."

"Oh, indeed," said Jeremy and he buried his face in his agenda to hide the laughter.

" I believe," said the newly-elected Chairman," that our President asked you all to go away and think. 'Ave you all done that?"

There was a general burble of concurrence around the table with the exception of Bobby, who seemed to be in a bit of a dream. He couldn't rid himself- nor did he wished to-of the memory of Tegan rearing up, astride him that afternoon and when his grandfather nudged him he answered, unawarely: "By Jove, yes!"

When he did become aware of his circumstances, he apologised profusely : "I mean, yes, actually-one or two.. pretty firm...things." and when he realised that the gestures he was making with both hands would have perfectly described Tegan's breasts, he hurriedly tucked his fists under his armpits.

Suggestions generally fell into two camps- coffee mornings and jumble sales and the annual church fair.

"But a festival, this time, "said Jenny Thomas," Not just the usual annual fete worse than death! Something to rival Port

Eliot or even take Edinburgh as a sort of ...paradigm!"

"'Scuse us," said Jago, assuming his thicker'n pigshit persona," but there d'be some a' we down 'ere as 'as difficulty wiv English- 'tis only a second language, mind- please elucidate!"

"You been to the Cornwall Show? Like that but with less bullshit!"

"Oh, a show- I knaws about they!"

"Festivals have been springing up all round Cornwall. Usually Beer or Cider Festivals which essentially mean a day-long piss-up but I reckon we could do something else- music and that?"

And she looked dolefully at Michael.

"You're not thinking of trying to do a Glastonbury, surely? Not with the roads round here." he replied. "I mean ,Glas screws up most of Somerset for days and they have motorways nearby. I mean, from what I've seen, an ordinary weekend in the summer round here is a nightmare, and that's just holiday makers- Add festival goers to that...Unthinkable, I mean, it's not hippies with sleeping rolls walking in any more. The least acceptable mode of transport is the surfers' VW van, even if you've never surfed. No, it's the rich trendies that come down from London in their Humvees , him and her, three brats and the nanny cum au pair cook! I mean, we fly in, not so much because we can do as because we'd never get there if we didn't. The crew are there days, weeks ahead!"

"No , I didn't mean quite that but there are local bands-" said Jenny.

"And a play, possibly?, Open-air of course, now that the Church Hall is no more..-we might even have it on the lawn out here.." Lady Olivia had been quiet, listening to the others but she was no longer well enough to act herself- something wrong with her back that was affecting her appetite- but she had been one of the founder members of the Players and wanted them involved.

"Yeah, but what!?" replied Jenny. "You tell me of a play with a cast made up of three octogenarian old ladies, a girl of fourteen and Jeremy as juvenile lead, and I'd jump at it. It's a perennial problem. And one of the octogenarians is going to have a hip done. " Jeremy smiled with embarrassment and decided not to minute the discussion too closely.

"How about scenes from Shakespeare?" It was Ashley. " I took the missus to sommat like at Stratford. Not a whole play but bits as we can manage. I mean, I'm no expert but... the Nurse and Jennyt ?.. and Prospero and Miranda- "

"And we could possibly do something from 'A Midsummer Night's Dream'." It was the first they had heard anything from the school's Miss Sutton and she had a lovely warm, low voice.

"With the children,,,"Everyone was looking at her. "As fairies...?" She stopped in confusion, whereupon Lady Olivia rescued her. "That's a lovely idea, dear."

"And weren't there sommat about bottoms?" Jago knew full well that there was; he just did not like to encourage too much involvement with Jenny. Years ago, they had had a fling and as a committed devotee of non-commitment, he did not like to be too prominent during her regular trawls through the village for a male actor.

" Right,!" the Chairman spoke. "We mustn't get bogged down in minutiae. Minutiae are the bane of committees. We'll set up a sub-committee for the Festival- Jenny? I presume you'll want to be in on that?"

"Well, I-" She didn't want to lose contact with Michael but found it difficult to avoid the obvious. "If we can have this young chap?" She knew Bobby's name full well but did not want to appear to be too eager.

"And...Jeremy-would you have you time for that?"

"Well..."said Jeremy, who found Jenny a tough cookie.

"Of course he will," said the Vicar .

"And me and Henry. I think we'd best keep control of the main event in the hands of the main committee?"

"Seconded." came the voice from the Admiral's armchair; he found Lady Olivia's dining chairs rather unforgiving on his piles and so had sought special permission to sit in the softer armchair.

"Thank you. Now, as to coffee mornings and jumble sales; do we need to have even more? Could we not simply ask the regular organisers if their profits, for the time being, went to the Church Hall fund?"

"See?" said the Admiral. "I said it made sense to have someone on the board who knows the score , even if he does come from Birmingham."

"Very kind, sir.-"

"If I may?"

Michael had been watching, in secret admiration and didn't like to interrupt, and he said so.

"But I don't know if Mr Treasurer.. I'm sorry, I've forgotten your name-?"

" Lake. Henry Lake."

"If Henry or anyone else, for that matter- has any idea of what the repairs might cost?"

"I'm no expert but I'd say hundreds of thousands-"

"Millions!" It was Jago who was experienced in costing the building jobs done around the village and who found no difficulty in multiplying up the likely expense for a whole Village Hall.. True, his estimates did tend to take in the reputed wealth of the customer, coupled with their knowledge, or otherwise, of small works.

"Yes." said Michael, "I tend to agree with...Mr.." He couldn't remember Jago's name either and several voices helped him out

"Jago"

"Absolutely. Jago. I think we'd be holding Village fetes

until the cows come home if we're going to rely on them to fund the new Hall. I hate to say this but there is really only one way- apart from robbing a bank- that we're likely to get this sort of money- and it's not out of place down here.

That's -!

"Smuggling, dear."

The cut-glass tones of Lady Olivia rang forth from the foot of the table.

"Yes. Smuggling." said Michael, "I'm afraid so."

"And smuggling drugs." said Lady Olivia by way of clarification

"And if we'm talkin' importin' stuff, then it has to be coke. People is growin' their own weed down these parts- same as everywhere else"

"We bow to your expertise, Jago" growled the Admiral , unable to keep the amusement from his voice.

"Not that I knows nothin' about it but I do hear said that coke, tis above seventy five grand a kilo this side of the Pond and what you pays for it over yonder could be anything,from nothing up to and including your life."

This threw an altogether different tone across the meeting. Then the Vicar spoke up.

"Do you think we can manage this without...err.."

"'Sin'? Is that was you were wondering, Vicar?"

"I was thinking more of breaking temporal rather than spiritual laws? Could we all end up in jug?"

They all looked at each other; nobody knew for sure but everybody had a pretty good idea.

"I think the answer's probably 'Yes'."said the Admiral. "They might be lenient on Olive 'n me on account of our ages but you lot..."

"Rather depends on who's sitting," offered Henry Lake. "But I think that it's a definite possibility."

"Then, shouldn't we offer everybody the chance to opt out before things get ...er...dubious."

It was young Bobby.

"Not that I want out-"he added quickly." Should be jolly good fun- I just felt we ought to offer it- like they do in that film. You know..? 'The Magnificent Seven'. Yul Brynner says to Robert Vaughn : "Go ahead ,Lee, you don't owe anything to anybody' and Robert Vaughn-remember,that black leather glove? He says-..."

Michael interrupted, in character" 'Except to myself' !"

A smatter of applause and laughter greets this and Jenny tries her luck ." I don't suppose you're free for the next three months? Rehearsals twice a week , evenings. "

"What's the play?" asks Michael.

"Whatever you want, darling. You choose."

"Sorry but...I can't commit."

"I know the feeling" echoes Jago.

"Oh, but does that mean you can't be involved? At all?.."asked the Vicar.

"Oh, no, no- I'm in on the project. One hundred per cent. It's just I'm not here all the time for your play."

"Nothing ventured..." said Jenny. " Damn! Where were we?"

"Costing the job," said Jeremy and Henry Lake together, both anxious to emphasize their involvement.

"Without being rude about my fellow builders," said Jago, temporarily discarding his role as old salt, "but if they think there's a bottomless pit o' cash, costs for labour and materials can spiral, 'specially if it's a council contract. It could cost millions and go on for years. They could look on it as the pension fund they never paid into . You just have to look at they new houses over wossname. Took twice as long, three times the cost and two of the plasterers took early retirement."

"Would you do that?" The question came from Michael.

Jago hadn't really thought of that. Years of guaranteed work, them accepting his estimates, no matter what? And then he looked round the table. Some- Jenny, Alf and less well, the Admiral and Lady Olivia, he had known all his life. Some , the lady teacher and the Admiral's boy- he'd only met yesterday. And the others, Ashley Pine and Henry Lake, the Vicar and his...what? 'partner', well, he knew them , they were..what? They were neighbours. These were the village, who the new hall would be for.

"No."

The sigh of disappointment was audible.

But then, Jago went on. "Not on me own! I'd be lyin' if I said I could. Bloody County, they'll 'ave ter do the road, the sewers and that hard-standing out the front- we'm not getting involved in land-slips and sewers, but if you wants,

I reckon that me and the boys, Nathan, 'H', the chippies and plumbers and electricians that we knows- works with all the time- I reckon us 'll make you a 'ansom 'all. One thing I will say though, or so I'm told, don't go snortin' that coke stuff with they new fivers- cuts your nose to buggery!"

"And...and.." It was Lady Olivia's voice which could be heard over the laughter.

"I know it's unlikely, but equally so, don't try to..'snort' I think the term is, with the very old white five pound notes. They're far too big, when rolled into a tube. Need a sniff like Jumbo the elephant .What we used to use..."And the whole room, with the exception of the Admiral, gasped audibly. " What we used to use was a very nice, if rather expensive antique silver tube thing that Asprey's used to make on the Q.T. for a rather esoteric clientele. They do say dear Princess Margaret had one. A real touch of class".

Chapter 9

The Festival sub-committee were happy to be getting on with something tangible. Jenny had executed a bloodless coup and quite simply taken the head of the long table at the back of the public bar of '*The Court'* at their first meeting. It meant that she should could keep her eye on young Bobby whom she had immediately seconded to her group. She had intended to keep him safe from the clutches of women, (other than her self) but had a terrible feeling that Tegan might have beaten her to it. Women sense such things. Obviously, their first priority was to get Michael to agree to do something.

"Possibly acoustic?" she had suggested to the committee before they had gone their own ways," Rather like that super Eric Clapton album, 'Unplugged'? "

But Michael had replied, enigmatically, :"Oh, no-if we are to appear then the Sword must appear , and if the Sword appears, I shall need power." And had further confused her by adding."I shall have to talk to the Angels." Fortunately, someone pointed out that Michael's band was called 'the Archangels' and that this was probably just an abbreviation.

Michael Donohoe had been born in Ireland, just outside Dublin, but, at the same time as the various members of what would become Ireland's most famous band- U2 -were, unknown to each other, being brought from their various birthplaces to Ireland's capital, so the Donohoes were leaving it for England, Bristol in particular. Michael's father worked in the aerospace industry and really, there was no other place to be at that time. Michael was a happy boy, singing around the house and picking out tunes on the upright piano that otherwise would have remained untouched in their front room in Westbury-on-Trym. And once they had recognised this natural bent, his parents sent him to the Cathedral School, where the routine of singing services every day, sometimes several on Sundays, meant that his musical skills were honed as his religious faith was strangled at birth.

While a Cathedral school may not be the same sort of hotbed of revolution and creative energy as the art schools of the late Fifties and early Sixties that had engendered the

Beatles, the Stones, the Kinks and their peers, it did produce kids who could all sing, had near-perfect pitch and who understood the difference in semi-tones and the importance of such knowledge. They didn't have to learn how to play in front of long-suffering fans; they could read and write music and the regime of singing not just the established canon but some modern ecclesiastical music as well , and not all by Rutter, five or six times a week meant that they had a grounding better than almost any other band in the limelight. They may not have been able to design their own album covers but their voices could be compared with those of the angels. Hence Michael and the Archangels. They spent two weeks and their hard-earned cash in the Sawmills recording studios near Fowey and were ready for the world. 'Michael and the Angels' was an inspired mixture of rock and ballad and soon was gaining a reputation, most especially 'Lady' which displayed Michael's remarkable range, from a comfortable falsetto to the warmth of his chocolate baritone.

Once they had got their first record deal with an independent producer who was then swallowed up by a mega-firm and then retired to a country estate, they were on the way. The success of their follow-up album, 'Songs of Angels', which included "Armageddon"and established their rock credentials, ensured there was no looking back and there were reports of actual physical fisticuffs in executives' offices in Kensington over who was going to sign what. That was more than twenty five years ago. The idea to change their names, or at least to give each other nicknames was greeted with mixed reactions. For Andy Parkes, Michael's oldest friend from Cathedral school and lead guitar, 'Andrew' was no great leap, but for Roger Cross, bass, and his brother Gary , their drummer, 'Raphael' and 'Gabriel' took some getting used to, and they were really only used in fun, or to annoy credulous journalists.

Everything had changed ten years ago once Michael had met Joanna; the birth of Jake followed three years later and of course, even more so, the previous year when she had succumbed to cervical cancer. The other three told the world that they were involved in their own projects and Andy even got as far as writing a few half-hearted songs but really they were all treading water, waiting for Michael to resurface. Instead, he had bought the Garden House, ensconced himself and the boy there , with Mrs G. a former primary school head mistress who had musical tastes of someone half her age as Jake's tutor/ nanny and was delighted to work for Michael. They were a comfy trio.

Chapter 10

"Lavatories".

"Out the back",explained Charlie, the landlord, who had seamlessly co-opted himself onto the Festival Committee by dint of the fact that they were meeting in his bar and he was serving.

"No- not <u>your</u> bog," said Alf, the milkman. " Fer the audiences. Tis the same every Regatta. Only just enough of them on the quay and then for some reason which, fer the life of me, I cannot understand, County goes an' locks them up half way through the festivities. Says tis too expensive to keep them open. Which is why the sea goes green round the back later on.. If we'm gonna 'ave thousands of visitors, we're gonna need more n' what we've got now and they've got to stay open! Bugger the cost! Otherwise, Charlie 'ere'll be swamped. Literally."

"And what about catering?" Henry Lake from the shop was a practical man. He had to be.

Many older people could easily remember when there had been more than a dozen shops in Porthwallow, providing everything everybody wanted, right down, as old

Mrs. Tonkin used to say, to 'a yard of knicker elastic.' Such haberdashery had been available in 'Chantal de Paris's boutique and coiffeuse, Branches in Paris, London and Rome', (or rather, Elsie Tom's hairdresser's and frock shop, as it was better known). Henry and his family did what they could in the shop but no-one could do everything. He had come down from Berkshire nearly twenty years ago with his wife Alma and their two daughters, Cheryl and Tina who could unfortunately have sat for the original Russian Matryoshka nesting dolls, three identical rotund ladies, the younger slightly smaller than her sister, while their mother was bigger again.

"When I say Berkshire," said Alma,"Nobody really knows where I mean but if I say we could and did wave to our dear Queen when she was in residence at Windsor, you get a better idea. I don't think she waved back."

"Harry did. I saw him" said Cheryl.

Alma was very chatty behind the till, which drove her daughters into a world of monosyllabic , if not silent communion. Unfortunately, the fact that they had taken over the baker's wares when the actual shop had shut , coupled with the confectionery (and papers) when the newsagent's went under meant that temptation was too near at hand and they had succumbed. Milk chocolate hobnobs, dunked into sweet tea, whilst devouring the Daily Mirror and Hello! with their eyes was their chief undoing and pass time. Henry was far too busy doing everything else to do anything about it, as he had discovered that it was easier to do it all, rather than have a blazing row withhis womenfolk in front of customers. . On the occasions when they did bestir themselves, he was pleasantly surprised.

He found his daughters' predilection for white ankle socks rather touching, which was worrying for, at 40 and 38 respectively , most people thought they were rather too old for them.

And he doubted the shop's capabilities to cater for an invasion.

"Do you think the pub can cope or should we think about mobile catering?"

"The least mobile anything we can manage the better. I mean, if we can do without any more vehicles than is absolutely necessary on the roads, the better" Ashley was being sensible again.

"We've done over a hundred at a sitting, regular," answered Charlie.

"But we could be talking thousands."

"Do you really think so?!"

"We have to hope so,"

"This may be silly,"said Bobby, who had noticed that Tegan who was behind the bar had moved towards their end and so wanted to make a good impression, "Totally out of left field, yah? But how about floating chippies? Like, I mean, okay, we get fish and chip vans yah? - they have mega ones down at Par Market, why not load them straight on to a fishing boat, or if that's too heavy- just the paraphernalia? The kit? Yah? The chip pans? And serve straight over the side- if we get the tide right. Like when we brought in the beer the other day after the storm-" Nobody said a word, "At least it's worthy thinking about?" They were all thinking.

Across the bar, Tegan gave him a quick thumbs up, which Jenny failed to notice.

She had also failed to notice the flinging open of the front door and the arrival of Letitia Butt, propelled by Cyril Oliphant. He had been the first and only one to go running to her once she had been installed by Joyce Dingle. Joyce was paid a minuscule retainer for which she was expected to be available whenever the old lady's whim took her. The cottage was to be lit, warm and welcoming with whatever fuel and food this may have necessitated provided out of Joyce's own pocket, as the retainer, paid in September had been spent by November. Mrs Butt's own children had given up on her long ago so now she normally expected Joyce's husband, Ken, to fetch her from whichever station she decided to arrive at, because taxis were deemed a prohibitive expense; the discovery that the Vicar's boy friend was prepared to fetch her, apparently for free, had sunk very quickly into her brain.

Cyril had helped her down stairs and in to the wheelchair- "rather too intimately" she had thought and they had now made a dramatic entrance, missed by almost everybody except Tegan, who asked what she could get them.

"I thought as much!" she boomed and the faces that had been turned in on the thought of floating chip vans now turned out to observe this monstrosity.

"Hello," said Jenny, bravely. "Mrs Butt. I didn't think you'd be down this time of year."

"Nonsense. Cyril. Park up this thing- don't forget the brakes- and get me a drink. A large vodka-

Absolut if they have bought some more, or Smirnoff'll do if not."

"Um, excuse me, Mrs Butt, but I'm temporarily out of funds - I was rather hoping ...-"

"Well, get them to stick it on my account.!"

"Uh-about that, Mrs. Butt." It was Charlie the landlord who had come down as soon as he had heard her voice.

"What now!?" she growled, menacingly.

"About your tab- you haven't paid the last one."

"What do you mean?"

"Just that. You left at the end of August without paying your account."

"I left Joyce to pay it.

"Yes but you didn't leave her any money."

"Same at shop," called Henry Lake, encouraged by the distance across the bar and the fact that someone else had introduced the subject. "There is a considerable bill that will have to be paid before I can let you, or Mrs Dingle on your behalf, or even this..er...gentleman'"(He meant Cyril whose tendency to fasten on elderly ladies had not gone unnoticed.) "here have anything more from the shop."

"Cyril" she pronounced," Take me home!"

"Aren't we going to try to find out what they're doing?"

"Take me home, or if you will not, I shall crawl unaided!" And she made a melodramatic attempt to rise from the chair

"Now, don't be silly!" Tegan was bustling round the end of the bar."If you'll keep an eye on our plotters of Cabbage Patch corner, "she said to Charlie,"I'll see Mrs Butt home,"

"Can I help?" asked Bobby, leaping from his stool.

"I'm sure an extra hand would not go amiss."said Tegan .And they had the spluttering old lady whose grand gesture had completely gone awry out of the door before anyone could say a word.

Jenny was miffed at losing Bobby, even if only

temporarily; she breathed deeply and asked: "So! Floating chippies, yes or no?"

"'Ang on a minute" It was Ashley Pine." Who were that?"

"Letitia Butt. Has that house on Fore Street. Needs a coat of paint..The house, not her- "

"I don't know," interrupted Jenny.

" Her husband was something quite big in Macmillan's government."

"And is she really flat broke?"

" Is she hell?! She owns a three storey maisonette in Knightsbridge, having just sold the one next door for five million."

"So what's this thing about not paying her tab?"

Henry from the shop explained: "She is the last, thank God- sorry, Vicar-, of that certain breed who felt that money and such matters were terribly non-U."

"Non-U?"asked Ashley.

"U and non-U? 'Us and not us.' If you were non-u, you were at least below the salt if not beyond the pale."

"Where?!" Ashley asked.

"Bugger me." said Alf. "Is it any wonder foreigners can't

understand we when us d'talk like that!"

"It seems in olden days, the housekeepers used to deal with it. Used to have to send a footman or something chasing round London, making sure she wasn't arrested for shop-lifting. Now she's just got a Portuguese maid, and that one goes home at night. I think Harrods bill her solicitor direct. Well, I've not got the time!"

"I don't like to see unpleasantnesses -they upsets me- no, I mean, physically."And he held out a hand that was still shaking. "What's the damage here? "

Charlie checked the till. "We're talking coupla hundred here. Weasel features, Cyril, used to add to it- said she said it was ok!"

"And the shop?"

"Not much change out of five hundred."

"Bloody hell!"

Ashley had delved into the inside pocket of his Barbour and produced a wad held together with a thick pink elastic band.. Most of them had never seen so many fifty pound notes.

"Look, if I settle now, just tell her it's been done but not who dunnit. But I'm not doin' it again."

"Are you sure?"

" I am. I hate to admit it, but she reminded me of my old mum."

Chapter 11

"Admiral?" Michael asked.

"Oh, call me Bobby, my dear fellow, or Robert if it's going to confuse things with the boy."

"Thank you. This may sound a silly request, Robert, but does the Navy still have landing craft?"

"Don't know about the Navy, don't know that we ever did- all we've got left as far as I can see is a few rubber ducks to play with in the bath. But the Marines, they probably need a few. I'll get on the old dog"

Michael looked perplexed, as did the others.

"'Dog and bone'? The old phone? I do think, in the light of what we hear from our cousins across the Pond, that all these new-fangled toys, wonderful that they might be, Email and ' social media'-whatever that might mean!- Honestly! Anti-social media, yes- all you see these days is people bowing in prayer with their noses up their phones- but after all the hoo-ha with Hilary Clinton and the Ruskies, I think the less we use these wonders the better. Sad you don't all do semaphore or Morse but if I may, can we stick to the old phone? And by that I do mean, the old one- the 'land-line'! Doesn't that sound impressive!"

"Excuse me." It was Alexandra, the little school mistress. Everybody else had forgotten her.

"I sign. If that might be of use. I don't know. I dive, you see. And we use it underwater."

The other pairs of eyes all regarded the young woman differently, especially those of Michael.

"I dive too."

"You must let me take you out," came the surprising reply.

"Aren't we getting a little ahead of ourselves?." Sandy and Michael lowered their mutual gazes, in what Michael was surprised to feel was pleasant embarrassment, something he hadn't felt for nearly thirty years.

"Now," yapped the little Admiral, "I doubt GCHQ are tapping into what us old farts are saying but as soon as their toys pick up one of their trigger-words from the ether, we could be 'swatted' in no time. Some bright spark in Langley catch so much as a mention of cocaine and they could send one of those smart bombs that comes in through the window, turns left at the dining room door, wipes its feet and blows us all to buggery. Scuse my French, dear. So we could send each other notes. I know for sure they aren't opening everybody's letters yet. What we need to know is where to get it from, how much it might cost at source, how we might raise that money- jumble sales and coffee mornings apart- Have you been to a Porthwallow bring-and-buy, yet, Michael? No? A pleasure in store. Then any suggestions as to how to get it across the Pond and how we're going to get it ashore. I imagine, though I'm sure Michael and even Jago, might be able to help here, the actual selling the ah- merchandise- won't be that difficult. I belief Rock runs on the stuff- that is, Rock the village over on the North, opposite Padstow where all the trainee hoorays go after their A levels-, not ah- the world of Rock-a-boogie.!"

"Don't you be so sure."

"So, let's get those telephones red hot in the morning."

As the meeting was breaking up, Michael found himself accosted by Sandy. He was not consciously trying to keep the world at bay so when she asked him if Jake shouldn't be at school, he found himself agreeing to her coming next morning to offer her professional advice. And possibly even talk about diving.

"The White House?"

Lady Vincent had recognised the heavy breathing even before the other had spoken and so kept it formal.

"Olivia, it's me."

"I'm sorry...' Me'?"

"Letitia Butt, of course. What's going on?"

"Well, we're going to do what we can to rebuild a hall."

"No-not that. Somebody has paid my tab"

"Good Lord!.How terribly kind-"

"No, it's not- now I have to carry money. Won't let Joyce have anything without. So bloody common! They actually came round this morning to tell me. Course, I wasn't out of bed and couldn't get a word of sense out of either of them. That's what comes of having incomers running the local businesses. Where are all the Cornish!?"

.

"Menadhu?"

The single word, as pronounced by the sepulchral tones of Hives the butler at the de Coverlet family home out on the headland was enough to make most people think twice before continuing.

Fortunately Lady Olivia knew the old chap well and ,on the excuse of powdering her nose-(before the meaning of that had come to evoke certain other indulgences), had shared many an illicit plum brandy in his pantry when her necessary presence at formal dinners had threatened to decline into her contemplating suicide.

" It's Olivia Vincent, Hives."

"Lady Olivia! What an absolute delight. You have made my day and if things continued unabated,
you will have made my week, if not my year."

"You old flatterer. Thing is, how is he?"

" I regret to say that old Sir Cosmo is with us only in body these days, ma'am. That power of attorney thing was signed just in time."

"And young Sir Cosmo?"

"He too is with us in body, I believe. I would hesitate to comment on his state of mind as I have not seen him in the flesh, as it were, for several days , It appears that there is a very popular series on the television, something to do with

Thrones and his is very much a tray-centric world at the moment.

"They arrive laden with his favourites at his living room door and the girl collects them, empty, or at least interfered with, later. We haven't heard a bell, so I'm presuming this imaginary world is keeping him more than satisfied than reality. I do believe there are breasts in it."

"Well, I'd hate to interrupt and, anyway, you probably are as well-informed as anyone about the family."

"You're too kind, Lady Olivia,"

"Quite simply, where are they all? The family, that is?"

20834

Alf, the award-winning milkman, was intrepidly working his way around the village, silently thanking the god of all milkmen that on that dreadful night, the best part of the village had been empty, the second-homers mostly in their first homes and even some of the indigenous who could afford it away skiing.

"Skiing!" Jago had mocked. "Nail a couple of meters of 4 by one to your work boots, rub on the old Vaseline and look out, piste, 'ere we come. And as for the Apres ski! Two pounds of yarg in a pot of scrumpy over a log fire and there's your fondu party!"

Alf stopped at the scar where the Hall had been and joined the little group of locals there, doing what they did the best, considering the job in prospect.

"Fuck me,!" said Hezekiah , rubbing his hands as he joined the group. "This could make us a bob or two."

"Nope!" snapped Jago. "None o' that, boy. We'm doin' it fer the community. Fer our families- and kids and that."

"Woss up with you? You ain't even married. You in't 'ad it away fer that long, you probably forgot where 'tis!" But he was the only one to laugh. The others realised that Jago was serious.

"If you don't want to work straight fer a change, "said Jago, "You can fuck off now. Us can find us plenty a donkeys to do the ' eavy work and they'm all prettier n'you."

"Don't get yer fuckin' knickers in a twist. I never said I was gonna fiddle' no invoices. Just said I fuckin 'could! So!" He looked at the others," We'm all workin' fer the Vicar now! "

And he couldn't help it; he paused with all the experience of the expert comedian. "Him and his boy-friend!"

"And we'll 'ave none of that neither!"

This time it was Alf. Alf rarely spoke so when he did, people listened. "Tin't funny. They'm good people, if n'you d' only take the time to get to know them. Good people. At last, you could 'ave something to work for that isn't just you an' your missus! "

"Wo'ss that, then?"

"The village!"

Out at the Garden House, there was a knock on the front door, a massive oak monstrosity that suited the Victorian pile. The nineteenth century sea captains of Porthwallow had been very successful and decided that they deserved houses that reflected their newly-earned wealth; sadly, it said little about their taste.

Alexandra Sutton was standing at the door when Jake opened it, this time dressed in a onesie that seemed to represent a panda.

"Hello," he said ,"you must be the school teacher."

"Hello," she replied "And you must be Jake."
"Not necessarily" he said, taking her hand and leading her into the magnificent kitchen."We may keep strange children as servants. And dress them as endangered wild species."
"And do you?"
"No. But you wouldn't know that immediately. Yes, I'm Jake. Michael- your young lady is here."

Michael was perched on a stool, drinking coffee.
"Hello- Coffee?"
"That's never her name, is it?" asked Jake
"Jake!"

A stern voice came from the other person, Mrs Guthrie, who obviously had a special tone for curbing her charge.

Michael introduced the women. Mrs. Guthrie pulled a face, not entirely as a joke.
"Well, if you are going to take him off to school, there will be no further need for me,"
"Now, Rose, you know that isn't true. When I get back on tour..."
"Won't I be coming with you?" asked Jake.

"Not all the time- and this isn't the time to discuss it. Sandy has come to see us and talk about diving."

"I can dive- Off the edge of the pool. Not the board. Not yet."

"This is possibly under water! Scuba! What's 'scuba' stand for?"

Like a parody of a performing child, Jake put his hands behind his back and adopting an American accent, said:

"Self Contained Underwater Breathing Apparatus! Michael's real good and is going -"

A cough drew him up short .

"Where are we?" asked Mrs Guthrie.

"I'm sorry" He leaned forward to Sandy and whispered, in the full knowledge that everyone could hear him.:"She doesn't like me using Americanisms."Then up, " Michael's really good."

"And who's 'she'? The cat's mother?"

"Mrs. Guthrie doesn't like me !"

"Now, Jake, that's not true!" Mrs G. was shocked.

"Jake!" This was a Michael Sandy had not seen before, stern and commanding."Stop it! He's only showing off.

Maybe this wasn't such a good idea."

"No, no. I'm sorry, Mrs G."And he pattered over to her and bowed and then pattered over to Sandy." I'm sorry, Mrs Sandy,"And bowed.

"*Mea culpa, mea culpa.* That's Latin, you know. Means, I'm sorry'"

"Actually," said Sandy. "it means :'my fault."

"Do you speak Latin too?"

"No, not really. And it's Miss Sandy."

"So, Miss Sandy. What do you want to know?" Again, the cod-American accent.

"Well,I thought we might do a few addings-up and takings-away."

"Addition and subtraction? Just arithmetic. Right. I'm not brilliant at long division yet but... "

Sandy handed him a note pad and fibre-tip pen but noticed he took his own A3 pad and pencil which he sharpened before facing her and, without taking his eyes off her, except to scribble, answered the questions which she read from a Government-issued text book that she had fetched from school..

"Nine plus three?"

"Twelve" Scribble

"Ten plus four?"

"Fourteen.". Scribble-

"Six plus seven?"

"Thirteen."And the little boy frowned a bit as he scribbled.

"Try something a bit harder- two hundred and twelve minus one hundred and three?."

Jake looked at Sandy, no obvious expression on his face.

"One hundred and six. "

She turned a few pages on.

"Three hundred and forty five minus one hundred and ninety two."

Again the frown and the scribble.

"One hundred and fifty three., I think"

"You think very well-you got them all right - can I see your workings?"

"Oh, I wasn't working out."

"What were you scribbling?"

"It isn't very good."

And Jake was right; it wasn't very good but it was a

perfectly passable sketch of a lady reading from a maths book, for a boy of seven.

"And you did this while you were thinking?"

"Yup!"

"Jake!" It was Michael.

"Sorry. I meant :'Yes'"And the little boy leaned forward to share his secret. "Michael doesn't like me talking American either. It reminds him of Joanna." Sandy looked up, to see Michael turning away quickly to look out of the window.

"Now, young man," It was Mrs Guthrie who had learned to know when to interrupt." I think it's time for a break. And there are some good things that the Americans gave us. Like marshmallows?"

"Right on! I'm allowed to say that. That's acceptable cos we're dealing with things American, namely marshmallows. In hot chocolate?" he asked.

Mrs Guthrie watched for the nod from Michael before agreeing.

"Do you like marshmallows in your hot chocolate, Miss Sandy?"

"Oh, not for me-"

"It's delish!"

"Too many calories. I shan't be able to fit into my wetsuit-"

"Oh, nonsense,"said the boy, before his father, for whom the bait had been cast, could reply.

" You have a really neat figure. A few marshmallows won't ruin it. "

"Well, thank you, Jake,"

"Then he went on. " Not completely.,"

But Sandy matched him:" Put that way, how could I refuse?"

"Well, Mrs Butt," said the Vicar, "You could always read some of your verse. You usually do."

The Reverend Uphill had not been able to avoid the summons any longer and so was visiting Mrs Butt; Jeremy excused himself on the grounds of having done his good deed for the week by picking her up from the station and depositing her at her house without strangling her.

"I do so want to be involved," she had wailed to him when he had refused to give her any sort of idea as to the project being planned.

"A poetry reading would involve you," he had said, carefully walking the slack rope between encouragement and downright lie. "Some people look forward to them. Lots, I'm sure."

"I don't ever remember seeing you at one?"

"Ah" replied Trevor, without thinking-" we usually hold 'Pinning the Tail on the Donkey' at about the same sort of time- have to cater for all tastes."

"I've nothing to read."

"Well, then, surely, now, at this time of coming-together-"

"It's hardly Harvest Festival, Vicar!"

"No but the community must grab this chance in both hands."

" 'Community'! That's the word they used for those unwashed dykes at Greenham Common! Or those nuns up at Sclerder. They're some sort of community, aren't they?"

"Carmelites, I believe. I have to admit, I haven't been very....'ecumenical' yet..."

"You've been here twenty years!"

"Twenty-one, nearly .The trouble is, with five parishes of my own, all supposedly Anglican, I don't get much time to

...ah..reach out to our Catholic brethren."
"And sisters!"
"Yes, but surely, now's the time to get writing. Did the landslide do nothing to inspire you?"
"Course not. I wasn't here, for a start. And by the time I did arrive, all was just.. mess. Don't know about you but I'm not inspired by mess!"
" Some people argue that Life is a mess,"
"Then perhaps I will."And she stopped. And thought. The said:" Yes, you're right. Think of dear Robert Herrick "Delight in Disorder" You know his church, of course? St George the Martyr at Dean Prior? Only up the road""
"I can't say I...." But by then, the old woman wasn't listening, lost as she was in her thoughts.

"'O little village beside the sea,
O beautiful village that's home to me " I can allow myself a little . .ah . . elasticity with the truth," she thought.
"'Thy poor dear privy innards gape" And then immediately: Victim of the dreadful rape." I don't think that's over-stating the case. Rather good ,that."

And Mrs Butt sat at her kitchen table, dictionary, rhyming dictionary and thesaurus spread before her school exercise book, pencils and sharpener at hand, pot of percolated coffee at her elbow. Letitia Butt was writing once more.

It is true that it was essentially the older generations of in-comers who rallied round the village leaders, in so far as there were any village leaders. By then, everybody who had wanted a taste of power had sat on the parish council for at least one term but with twelve separate councillors, it basically meant that there were twelve separate political parties and no on-going ethos.

The Cornish are essentially Liberal and had all come together under David Penhaligon and a bright future had been smashed the day he died; when the Lib-Dems committed hari-kiri on that day in 2010 when they joined the Conservatives as inevitable future whipping-boys, taking all of the pain, none of the gain, the future looked bleak. And it is only the hyperactive squeakings of a few busy-busy Lib-Dem County councillors that keeps the

Duchy from sinking into blue oblivion, remarkable only in the fact that some of the Tory Bigwigs with younger children have actually started taking holidays here.

While the doctors might have been seen as leaders in the past, none of them lived locally as they had to serve three other very differing communities in their practise. The young Head of the primary school was so good at his task that he has given another to run as well, so had no time.. And although the Vicar did have other churches, their congregations were thin indeed and, after all, he did live in Porthwallow. So, with Lady Olivia, whom few knew but everyone had heard of and the Admiral, a national figure who had retired to what had once been a second home but now become his first, the Vicar looked about himself and was frightened.

"I think" he said to Jeremy that night in bed," I think I'm sort of in charge."

Chapter 12

Trevor had never really felt 'in charge' even when he had been Head, (and only full-time member) of the Classics Department. True, he had had a couple of fading historians under him who taught Class. Civ. to Years 6 and 7 but all of the language work had been down to him. And, as he would say on the occasions when, consumed with self-pity, he thought back, it was down to him that no more Latin, let alone Greek was taught in that corner of Droitwich and what little was known about the Golden Age had been learned in translation.

The fact that he was a Classicist at all was a sort of happenstance. At school in Kent, he had been fairly bright and the confusion of hormones that had been adolescence had pointed him, like so many gay young men, towards the Anglican church. He loved the bells and the smells and even the music, from its ethereal evensongs to its more muscular Nineteenth-century hymns that they belted out every morning in Chapel, with even the thirteen year olds trying to sing bass like their idols in the Sixth Form; it had been the College chaplain who had suggested that the easiest way to get an Oxbridge place was to read Divinity. Even then, in the Sixties, numbers studying Greek and Latin were on the wane and so his teachers were delighted that they might at least have one students to make their lives worthwhile; when Trevor managed to persuade his friend, his only friend, Roger who didn't smoke or drink or brag about how far up the scale of one to ten he had got with 'that bird last night' and who was fat and wore glasses, to do Latin and Greek with him their cups runneth over.

Despite the two-to-one tuition, Roger only got three Es and ended up at Hull. Trevor, straight As, on the advice of his teachers, applied for Balliol College, Oxford, failed to get in there but was mopped up by the dons at the minor college whose High-Table silver was on loan from Balliol, land on which it stood owned by St Johns and dons drank sherry from plastic carboys which they kept on their bookcases, starting on the stroke of twelve noon. And he had loved it

.

An average 2:2 but in Classics had meant that the teaching world was almost his oyster- possibly his scallop, and the job in Droitwich seemed like an answer to his prayers. But occasional sexual skirmishes with members of both sexes amongst his colleagues had all proved pretty non-commital and fairly unexciting and it was this loneliness which had driven him to that folk club where the music was painful, the coffee dire and the clients troglodytic. All except Jeremy.

As their tentative relationship flourished, his life at school declined and when a teen-aged girl had first of all asked him what the fuck good was Latin and then told him to:" Get a life, Mr. Uphill" that he had handed in his notice and applied for training for the priesthood with the Church of England.

His four-year curacy had been purgatory in an inner-city parish in Birmingham partially because he and Jeremy were not allowed to share the curate's digs and partially because , for what was supposed to be a multi-cultural society, he had never met a more bigoted bunch, irrespective of race. When a perceptive bishop had had one of his regular little chats and offered him Porthwallow, "And probably two or three other little churches-lovely buildings- very popular with weddings- the old codger we've got there is on his way out, thank the Lord- no, I mean that in a caring way- "

he jumped at it and gradually the village had come to accept him and to accept Jeremy for who they were, a loving couple, far happier than a number of those in so-called orthodox relationships in the place.

Porthwallow was no different from the other little villages that clung to the south Cornish coast and it was all down to individuals to make or break them. It would be too easy to brand them all with the name of tourist traps, pretty old fishermen's cottages whose very lack of planning made them all the more attractive. Some, like Fowey and East Looe were probably too big to be called 'villages' as they suffered from the same infection that was blighting Newquay in the north and St Ives in the west, that of farmers, tired of a hard life making a living on these cliff top farms that their children didn't want, selling their fields to developers who threw up dozens of new houses without a thought as to where the people who were to live in them were to come from, where they would find work, go to school, buy their food, see the doctor and , ever increasingly, be buried- or at least dispatched from in the direction of the crematorium which at times was so busy that one party queued behind the previous and in front of the next and more than one mourner has found himself surrounded by people he did not know ,singing hymns and praying for the soul of someone he had never met.

In fact, it was the opposite . The few new houses that had been built as a sop to the locals had been snapped up; but they are on the outskirts , a hefty hike if you wanted to go down into the old village and an even heftier one coming back, laden with push-chair, several children under two, the dog and the shopping from ASDA whither you had been on the bus which seemed to offer an hour-long mystery tour when covering the five miles.

The beautiful old cottages, a few yards from the bus stop, stood empty for most of the year until those few weeks when the owners, or those who had hired them invaded.

" Olivia Vincent?"

"Ah, Lady Olivia!" The unmistakable tones of Hives at the other end of the phone caused Olivia's heart- if not to leap, then certainly to perform a little skip. This was no school-girl 'pash' but the thought of possible progress was exciting. And it caused such a comforting resonance down in her abdomen.

"Hives! Any progress?"

"Young Sir Cosmo would be delighted if you would come to luncheon tomorrow, if that is if you are free. I think the television program must have taken a break as we are to lunch in the dining room. It is still too cold for the conservatory."

"Do tell Sir Cosmo I shall be delighted, as long as I can get Pete to run me over."

"I beg your pardon?!"

"Oh, I mean, drive me to Menadhu. I don't imagine there is great call on his taxi at this time of year. If at all.. ."

"We could send a car, ma'am, I am sure."

"No, no-must support local enterprises. But if you have someone who could bring me back... I gave up driving when I passed eighty."

"Are congratulations due for a recent event?"
"No, no- months ago. I no longer make a song and dance about such matters- No longer can!"
"Sir Cosmo asked me to enquire, if you were good enough to accept our invitation, as to whether there was any thing that you do not eat? Have you discovered any allergies or aversions? They seem to be the 'in' thing?"
"Well, I never was very fond of tapioca. 'Frogs' spawn' we used to call it. I used to stick it up my knickers at school."
"I can assure you, my Lady, that there will be no sign of tapioca in tomorrow's menu and your knickers can remain inviolate."
"Thank you, Hives."

Although it was not as widely known as her thespian tendencies, Jenny Thomas was also a witch
" None of your bloody Harry Potter rubbish, darling."

She was trying to attract Bobby Hawkins by common or garden allure, aided by a few of her own specialities.
"My God, if I had a .." She searched for something supremely small. " A groat for every time I've been asked if

I went to Hogwarts, I'd be doing very nicely thank you."

Bobby had been made well aware of the fact that she was wearing only a poncho of sorts by the very evident activity of what ever might normally have been restrained by undergarments beneath. While not large, Jenny was a well-rounded woman and very well aware that young chaps like Bobby were unlikely to have experienced such a mature physique. Such knowledge did not help his attempt to understand white magic.

"It starts with the trees, darling. I know they call us 'tree-huggers' but that in't all we hug!"

She wasn't certain as to whether to play the 'femme fatale' or the rustic lovely.

"You must have been up in the woods?"she asked.

"Yes, we used to play up there all the time- every summer- not now so much- not in this weather."

"Well, there's trees up there that are magic. Definitely."

" Is that why the Man who Lives in the Woods...er.. lives in the woods?"

"Who?"

"You must know. Tegan says he's real."

"Oh, you must mean old Jack. Yes, 'Course 'e'es real. Some sort of relative, I think."
"That's what Tegan said. I didn't know you two were related?"
"Most of the village is related to each other, one way or another- one side of the sheet or the other. So, you been seeing a bit of Tegan?"
"Just about everything that there is to see," thought Bobby, but replied "Yes, she's been showing me.."Jenny looked at him sharply. ".around."
"A lot to see?" she asked, ambiguously.
"More than I thought."
"Well," she said, trying to ignore the suspicions that were looming. She sat back and inspected him, as a prospective buyer might do a colt.
" So. And what are you?"
"I beg your pardon?"
"What sign, or month- or, if you know it, birthstone?"
"I'm end of June- Cancer."
"A pearl. Ah. Shame. I don't have any- not the real thing."
"Don't worry."

"No, it's just that I like to give crystals to...*And here she looked at him," 'special people' -"
"Oh, I'm nothing special," he said, defensively.
"You could be."And she shifted along the bench towards him.
"Oh, no-." He recognised a possibility here if he played his cards right- or simply laid his cards down there and then on the table- but didn't want to confuse the issue. Anyway, he had only been able to get hold of one condom- the only one left in the dispenser in the gents at the pub, despite having paid for two-, and he wanted to be prepared next time he saw Tegan. Henry and Alma wouldn't sell them in the shop; they wanted to keep their girls out of the way of temptation. Another example of love being blind.
"You're very kind" said Bobby. "But I have to go. I promised Gramps...."
"Oh. Very well. We have plenty of time."

As business was always slow in the winter afternoons, Charlie was happy to give Tegan time off to continue showing Bobby around.

This time, their tour had briefly stopped at the old blockhouse but as it was unheated, stony on naked flesh and Bobby still only had the one condom, they did not stop long .

"Next time, " Tegan said, climbing back up the path, " we'll go out the the churchyard and I can show you my family's graves. Granny Phyllis's is very comfy."

Lady Olivia got out of the old taxi, only to discover that she did not have any money.

"Dun'ee worry, milady," said the old driver." I knows where you d'live! Me an' the boys'll be roun' dreckl'y'!" and he drove off laughing in a shower of gravel.

The door was opened by a very slight maid who bobbed a curtsey before gesturing towards Hives who was looming.

"Ah, Lady Olivia! What an absolute pleasure, as always. Monica, this is Lady Olivia Vincent, young Sir Cosmo's'... aunt? is it, Lady Olivia?"

"Probably some sort of cousin, more likely, but I get lost in 'seconds' and 'thirds' and 'twice times removed.' How do you do, Monica? Do you like it here at Mena dhu?"

"Yes, mmm."She lowered her eyes and then glanced at Hives for direction.

"Well, trot on and help cook. I imagine luncheon will be required in about half an hour."

"Yes,sir."

"Ah" And Hives raised a very long forefinger,"remember? I am not a knight!"

"No, s- Mr Hives,"

"We'll make a maid of you yet.", whereupon she scuttled off to the depths of the big house.

"New staff, Hives?"

"Rather a tricky subject, Lady Olivia. You will remember Emily, no doubt?"

Lady Olivia gestured as though weighing two bowling woods, one in either hand., in front of her own almost imperceptible bust.

"Exactly. Sadly, old Sir Como has, it seems, always been, how can I put this other than 'a breast man' and as he lost his faculties- senility is a terrible thing- so he lost any sort of self control and would, with no warning, grasp Emily and look expectantly."

"Poor thing,"

"It was upsetting for the girl as well,"

"I was meaning the girl," said Lady Oliva.

" And it looks as though young Sir Cosmo has inherited something of ..ah..this...ah...inclination so before things got..out of hand, as it were, I suggested to Emily that she look elsewhere and we could give her the most outstanding of references. Poor Monica will never, I fear, have such worries."

They went in to young Sir Cosmo, an incongruous figure of about fifty in black patent leather shoes, dress trousers, a maroon velvet smoking cap and jacket covering a T-shirt bearing the Rolling Stone Hot Lips logo. His ginger hair was long while his straggly beard had almost as much grey as ginger.

Over an excellent lunch of local oysters, lamb from the estate farm and peaches from the orangery, Lady Olivia explained the purpose of her visit; Cosmo's first reaction was: " Sadly, Olivia, you know we have no money," but after she had explained that such was not the purpose of her visit and that she wanted to know if, between them-and they included Hives in this- they could come up with some member of the family who might have some influence somewhere, he became quite enthusiastic.

"Well, young Philip is in the F.O. somewhere but talking of Colombia- we are talking of Colombia, I suppose? Eh, Hives? Cocaine? Colombia?"

"And Peru and Bolivia, too, I believe, Sir Cosmo."

"Dunno, but I tell you something; back, I dunno- thirty years- I was still in London. About '85- When Mick and Bowie did their version of 'Dancin' in the Street', remember? No? - anyway, I used to go to this club?

"You? Member of a London club?" Lady Olivia was surprised, " Not Pratt's, I suppose"

"No,no" said Cosmo, dismissively. "A Pole Dancing club, somewhere near the Windmill, it was- you know about these places, Auntie?"

"I have an idea-"

"You mustn't touch but you pay by stuffing money- notes you know, down whatever little bits and bobs they've got on. Bloody expensive, cos they expect fifties!"

"I believe it was one of the reasons that your father called

you home, Sir Cosmo."
"You make me sound like some sort of dog off the leash, Hives!"
"You gave us that sort of impression, too, sir."
"Anyway. Where was I? Oh, yes- Pole dancing- well, it's not exactly a team sport but it can attract an appreciative..ah.. select audience and more than once I met this chap who...let's say, had very similar tastes to me. We got chatting, between performances, is it were... and he was over here on a scholarship, from Columbia- yes- Economics.Up at Oxford by day, possibly, but he was down in Town around the back of the Windmill most nights! Very popular because he usually had freebies of the old national export and was very keen to share them out. Now, to be quite honest, I have no idea whose side he was on- over there the good guys and the baddies seem to swap sides daily and don't have white hats to help- but you know, I might just have a number... or a card. Somewhere.- they're often very keen on swapping cards- a lot of business get done at these places you know- real business and not just as a euphemism. I'll look it out.

"Otherwise, as I say, there's young Philip but, as you know, with young Philip, the least said the better. He has very nearly caused ...what's the word?,.. 'incidents' everywhere he has been posted and it's only because they were so extraordinary that nothing could be done. Except keep moving him on from embassy to embassy.

"I'm sure he never realised what he had done, eh, Hives?"

"I believe he takes after his uncle in that, Sir Cosmo."

"What? Oh." Though he did not really understand.

Chapter 13

Philip de Coverletwas a car. Almost always had been, ever since Noddy's little red car had come into his life, going 'parp, parp, parp' all those years ago and taken it over. He too had been a Morris Minor when young, with a red soft top and white sides, and he too went 'parp, parp' and, once he had learned the proper way to do it, drove himself around the house and the estate at Menadhu.

" I am slowing down. I am stopping. I am putting on the hand brake and switching off."

Often behind the sofa in the main sitting room.

They thought he would grow out of it but instead he simply became more and more prestigious cars. When he first saw the James Bond films, he was an Aston Martin with a throaty roar for a while but did not enjoy it; he got nowhere with girls, anyway. So he reverted to being whichever of the fleet of ageing Rolls Royces that sat in the stables at Granpa Cosmo's old house that currently took his fancy.

Not every primary school, even in the flexible Seventies , could cope with this sort of behaviour. Eventually they found a very expensive Prep. school near Ascot who would not try to change this infatuation; in fact, the Head, who wore tailored tweeds that were a mixture of orange and purple, and smoked Balkan Sobranie cigarettes said that they liked to encourage individuality in their charges. The fact that little Philip sat motionless and passive throughout lessons and only came to life when they allowed him to switch on his ignition at the end did not seem to faze any of the young teachers.

Philip passed Common Entrance with flying colours, much to everyone's surprise, despite the assertion from the Head that it was never in doubt. The Public School that had reared his family for generations forced him to be a little more 'normal' because some teachers, the scientists in particular, would take off House Points for misbehaviour and the House Prefects would see to it that Philip stopped. "How can it be 'misbehaviour'?" argued a more pedantic prefect."He isn't behaving at all!"

It had been hoped that he would join the steady if irregular procession of de Courtneys to Christchurch, Oxford but he was being a particularly precious Hispano-

Suiza with the roof down on the day of the interview and the dons who followed in the footsteps of Charles Ludwig Dodson turned this eccentric down.

Cambridge didn't, and it had been at Cambridge that a certain don who thought he recognised genius when he saw it, tapped him on the shoulder one day and invited him to join the Foreign Office.

It was an ideal environment for what some called 'eccentricity' and other 'insanity'. The British upper class usually found a suitable niche for such individuality somewhere, while other nations, such as the French and the Russians who had eliminated their aristocracies, looked on in envy. There, the deranged had become revolutionaries and had tended to liquidate the upper class first and then each other; in Britain, it was only the really dangerous who had been locked away- often in a darkened room on a distant part of the family estates with a devoted man-servant; otherwise, they were left to run free, occasionally actually in the government as members of Parliament, more often in the Civil Service, in Philip's case, the Foreign and Commonwealth Office. True, the number of embassies left for him to be shuttled between were fewer and farther between than they had been but it amused the mandarins among the upper echelons of Whitehall to appoint him to some of the less dangerous spots as Intelligence *attache*, usually a thinly-disguised euphemism for 'spy' in the knowledge that he would be bribed, cajoled and even, if he was lucky, seduced into giving up our secrets when all the while he was worried about his cam-shaft timing.

It was pure 'karma', 'kismet', serendipity, call it what you will, that Philip had only recently become, if not Our Man in Bogota. then certainly one of our men there, currently masquerading as a Nissan Qashqai.

Jim, Jenny Thomas's boy, was steaming across the Caribbean .

Petty Officer James Thomas (he was the son of Jocky Thomas, the deep-sea fisherman rather than the current long-distance lorry driver) had joined the Navy as soon as he could, as soon as he had left school. It offered him all that living with a single mother did not, most of all security and a living wage.

Early on, he used to send money home but he never got an appreciative reply and often no reply at all. She was obviously coping somehow, and he did like to think too deeply about 'how'.

But Jenny was very proud of him, in her own way and found it very amusing that his ship, HMS Runcorn, one of the River class of minesweeper, was employed on fishery patrol and to counter drug-runners!

"If he does catch us, I'll give him a good smack!"

It was no wonder that, having been born on Trafalgar Day, October 21st 1930, that little Bobby Hawkins had been given the middle name of 'Horatio'. His mother, on her bed of pain, had had a considerable struggle to stop her husband having him christened 'Horatio' first off but a few strategically placed tears had saved the day. But the boy was a devotee for life. He would walk around with one arm stuck up his jumper and a patch over one eye, until he read that Horatio had only lost the sight but not the actual eye. After Britannia College, Dartmouth, he could quote the order for battle for the ships of the line at Aboukir Bay,

Copenhagen and ,of course, Trafalgar and what was more, had thoroughly immersed himself in the admiral's scandalous life with Lady Emma Hamilton and her husband, Sir William.

One leave, in the mid 1960s, he had joyously retraced the 1799 victorious route of Nelson, Emma and Sir William, a curious *menage a trois,* all the way from Naples to London after the victory in Egypt *via* some of the more riotous of European capitals with a particularly obliging WREN taking the part of Emma. They ignored the absence of a Sir William. After all, he had only ever watched the original. Robert tried to explain to his wife that he was inspecting submarine installations in NATO bases but when she got a postcard from Switzerland, she smelled a rat.

Bobby Hawkins had always had an eye for the ladies but when his wife threatened to divorce him if he did it again, unless she was given the role of Lady Hamilton and his WREN transferred, he, unlike Nelson, realised that discretion was the better part of valour.

But the spark of romance had remained, which was probably why he rose above his contemporaries at

Admiralty House. Theoretically, any Naval officer can make it to Admiral if he can survive the boredom. Those last few steps, however, to Admiral of the Fleet, took imagination. It also took a breadth of knowledge which was why the young Captain spent as much time as he could with his various pursers and, eventually, Logistics Officers, as they were the planners of the Navy. He loved a plan.

'Dapper' could have been coined for him and he wore his beard a neatly-trimmed snow white which went with his blue peaked cap to perfection. There is a strange thing about seafarers' blue peaked caps- those worn by fishermen become flaccid, grey and stained; those by 'yachties' and retired naval officers remain pristine.

He had had an idea and had called all the elderly mobility scooter owners to a meeting in the village's Reading Room.

This place was one of only a few survivors of what had been a considerable movement in the Nineteenth century. Some of the more affluent villages upcountry had quite commodious premises .consisting of several rooms, for billiards and table tennis,and these developed into the village hall. Once called 'working men's reading room', the first part of the name had been lost to mass unemployment subsequent to the Great War while the second to mass hysteria subsequent to the move for sexual equality, Porthwallow Reading Room had really been a haven for those fishermen unable to sail because of the weather where they could spend their time out of their cottages away from their wives between the pub's opening hours. Some argued that it also acted a quite an important contraceptive.

The old folk were seated around the table, the lucky ones on chairs, the others- the more sprightly or the latecomers- on benches and this had been a snag that the Admiral had not foreseen, leading to all sorts of feeble jokes about 'getting one's leg over.'

"Right," said the old matelot, "as you may know, we're planning some sort of a shindig to try to raise some money to help rebuild the Church Hall."

"What?! What's 'ee say?" asked Mrs Barrie, ninety -three next birthday.

"Oh, turn it up." said Rodney Collard, a mere eighty-seven.

"What?"

And Rodney leaned across her withered bosom- which was what she had wanted all along -and turned up her hearing-aid.

"She never remembers," he apologised to the assembled crew, most of whom tittered.

"Right. Are we getting through to you now?"

"Oh, yes, thank you, Very nice."But her false teeth clattered some more," But I missed what he said to begin with. Forgot me volume."

" I was thinking of something rather like the Maypole. Or the Furry Dance, but to suit us. An event to raise money."

"Well, don't look at me for money. How they can expect you to live on a hundred and twenty five quid a week is beyond me. Mrs Queen couldn't. Us shouldn't 'ave ter."

There was a real danger that she had set a fox running as heads started to nod, and so Robert used his best poop-deck voice.

"Ladies!". They shut up. "And gents. I have an idea that we oldies-'

"Who's he callin' old?!" Kath Greaves, eighty nine.

"And not so-oldies can do."

"Well as long I dun't 'ave ter dance."said Mrs Barrie. " Not no more. I give up after me ninetieth- you remember, girl? "

"I assure you,"said the Admiral,"None of us will have to dance," A mutter of relieved approval, "Not in the strict meaning of the word. We shall simply have to follow my leader"

"But I just told 'ee, boy, I'm not so good on me pins."

"No- not on foot, I believe that you will have noticed- the more observant among you- that we each of us drive a mobility scooter."

"Ais" said Mr. Collard,"And we'm all tryin' to park as near 'ere as possible and 'tis a right old bugger-up. Tis worse'n when Bookers is deliverin' to the shop an' that's sayin' sommat."

Again the admiral had to raise his voice to nip the budding conversation.

"Yes-indeed. The idea is to involve our -ah- vehicles. What I have in mind is POEMS- that is, Porthwallow Over-Eighties Mobility Squad .".

That did set the tongues wagging, even if the ears were

not all capable of hearing what was being said, so the Admiral decided to call the meeting to a premature close and let them think about it. It was moments like these that Lady Olivia knew she should miss

Chapter 14

The Vicar sat alone in his beautifully carved seat in the choir stalls at St Wallow and allowed his gaze to wander over the magnificently muscular old oak roof above him, product of local shipwrights in the thirteenth century. The ribs of roof echoed the bare bones of a ship He often performed evensong this way; eyes wide open, the old words coming automatically to him as he gazed in wonder at the marvels of man. Some times Jeremy would sit in the stalls opposite and watch his friend but today he had allowed himself to be persuaded to take Mrs. Butt back to Bodmin station, as she had decided that there was nothing obvious for her to do in the village and that she was warmer and more comfortable under the charge of Maria, her Portuguese maid of all tasks and with her Harrods' deliveries on tick at hand. Her return journey to the station was even more convoluted than her arrival in that she and all her luggage had to be steered across the bridge over the rails as the train up to Town, obviously, went in the opposite direction and therefore on the other rails to that of the down train. Had it been possible, she would have insisted on it changing track, at least for the section through Bodmin Parkway station-

"There are points and things ,aren't there? Surely? Turn-tables and such things?" but Jeremy feigned ignorance while, as soon as she saw her, the poor woman who had helped Mrs Butt on arrival hid in the staff lavatory and pushed her younger colleague out.

"Pretend you're Romanian and don't understand." she hissed

Unfortunately, Romanian was one of the many Balkan tongues that Mrs Butt had picked up either on her travels or in her studies, so when the man muttered:

"Sorry-no understand. I- Romanian." she replied with :"Cum va namiti?" and he had no idea that she was asking his name.

"The man's a fool. There's no point in them sending us their idiots. We have plenty of our own. I had heard that the Romanians had a particularly good reputation. This one won't improve it.."

Fortunately, she had decided to leave the wheelchair in Cornwall and buy herself another for London; she had noted with envy and interest the variety of electric scooters that seemed to whiz around the village in spite of the detritus and could just imagine herself in something similar bombing along the pavement of the Brompton Road, straight into Harrod's.

Meanwhile back at the church, Trevor's reveries were interrupted by the southern door crashing open and a number of unlikely visitors entering.

"This'll do us. Tis 'ansome." Jago led the way, followed by Nathan Treglown, Steve Baker, the farmer and Hezekiah Pemberthy .

"Fuck me, I'd never thought about this place."'H' was not cowed by the majesty of his surroundings. His profanity was like a physical pain to Trevor, listening in the dark.

"Well, when was the last time you was in 'ere?"
"Dunno- when we buried Mother, I reckon-they takes most a the stiffs straight up the Crem these days, dunnum?. An' what weddins we do 'ave is out they... 'fuckin'....big 'otels."

Trevor had a switch for his microphone there beside him in his pew. Without raising his head, he flicked it and said, in as deep a voice as he could manage:
"Hezekiah Pemberthy!"

Almost in chorus, the four men reacted to what seemed to be a supernatural emanation.
"Fuck me!"
"No, that's quite enough!" The Vicar stood up , bowed to the cross on the altar, took off his stole, kissed it and turned to his congregation who could now see where the voice had come from.
"Everyone is welcome to the house of God but only if they behave. 'H', I will not have your habitual blasphemy, especially in this place!"
"Sorry, vicar, but you did give we one 'ell.. "

Jago coughed and hit 'H' who corrected himself.
" Er- One 'eck of a shock. An' I in't one ter quibble but I

didn't think 'Fu-" and he stopped and incredibly, used a euphemism- "'the F. word' was blasphemy. Profanity, yes but blasphemy? Tin't nothin' again' God. Anglo-Saxon it may be. Rude an' coarse, yes- an' I'm the first one to 'old me 'and up and say I'm rude and coarse- but in't that just it?- what tis all about. Your religion? The 'immaculate contraption-"

The Vicar corrected him.

"'Conception'-"

"Ais, 'conception'. In't that the 'ole point? God didn't fu- 'Ave 'is way._. Not wi' Mary. Not like old Zeus and Jupiter- they seemed to be at it all the time-Showers of gold and like a swan? How the 'ell- 'eck you does it like a swan, buggered if I knows-"

Jago didn't even bother to apologise. They were all rather surprised.

" But God left that to the 'Oly Ghost, din't 'e? Or old wossname- Angel Gabriel, wasn't it? So there was no- er..Oh, there's gotta be a word fer 'fuck' that is acceptable in polite society?"

"Good Lord- I never realised we had a philosopher in our

midst!"said the Vicar, only slightly jokingly. 'H' was slightly hurt.

"I d' read books, Vicar. Not just comic books neither."

"Well, I must apologize, Hezekiah. 'Copulate' might do. "

"Copulate? See ? There's none o' that in your whole..wossname... doctrine?"

"There is. In the wedding service. First thing, nearly. Look it up."

"'Ere," It was Nathan who interrupted. If Nathan had something to say, it must be worth saying because it was a very rare occurrence. "We'm 'ere for the play-actin', not all this....teasy...tin't 'Mastermind'!

"'Play'?" asked Trevor. "First I've heard...?"

"Mentioned it at the first meeting. " said Jago

"I didn't think we'd agreed..."

"If we don't get on,' twill never 'appen, specially if n' we leaves it all to Jenny. She's all mouth, that one-"

"Well, you should know," said 'H', before he could help himself

Jago just looked at him. And then went on,

"No, see, Vicar, what it is, tis where'd we re'earse? The 'all

is all down the 'ill and we all 'as council 'ouses and they rooms is tiny-"
"I got a barn," added Steve.
"Yes but tis open on four sides and full o' winter feed jus' now. So we got to thinkin,'"
"Where's there a empty space but that's indoors. "said H."Twas my idea. Never thought you'd be usin'it."
"It is really what I'm here for." Trevor tried not to be annoyed.
"What? "asked Nathan,"Weekdays an' all.?"
"Morning and Evening service. Every day. "
"What? All on your own?!" They were all amazed.
"Usually. There was an old Cornish vicar, back in the Nineteeth century, up near Bude, he used to allow his cats- and a pet pig- to follow him to church - there was no-one else- all the locals were Methodists, see? He excommunicated a cat for killing a mouse on a Sunday."
"But can we use that bit at the back-?" Nathan gestured to the space behind the pews beneath the belfry at the back of the nave.
"We only ever get enough to fill that bit at Christmas. And

funerals. Or big weddings from upcountry. Second-home owners- What do you want to do?"
"You remember I mentioned that bit in Midsummer Night's Dream?"
"The Mechanicals?"
"Ais- well , we may not 'ave weavers an' bellows menders an' all but we got chippies, an' painters, plumbers- and basic idiot labourers, like me..."
"Hey," Hezekiah interrupted." You know we said we was going to try to get Charlie to come and do that old chap?"
"Quince?"
"Ais but look- Vicar's already 'ere half them time- he's old...why not get him?"
"Vicar?"
Which was how Trevor Uphill, the Vicar of St Wallow came to play the carpenter , Peter Quince, in the Porthwallow Memorial Festival.

Cyril Oliphant had spent most of Letitia Butt's stay trying to make himself invaluable to her so that she might give him money but whatever he did do was deemed unremarkable by Mrs Butt, the sort of acts of kindness that she would expect of anyone associating themselves with her.

Oliphant was an unusual name. leading to all sorts of name-calling at school but none of the teachers could find it in them to defend him. They thought him a sneak rather than a victim and this sort of judgement followed him everywhere. Even his parents found him obnoxious. He tried his hand at several professions but simply could not hit it off with his employers or colleagues. And there were the incidents. In the end, they decided to make him a small allowance so that he could go and live in their cottage in Cornwall and stay out of trouble.

That evening, as he stood at the foot of the wreck of Fore Street. he worked out in his mind where he might best try next. Now that Mrs Butt had gone, the only other inhabited building at the bottom of the hill was the shop and there was nothing that he could do there. Then he noticed Jago Hocking and Ashley Pine in conversation as they headed out towards the cliff. Curious as to what might be bringing them together and what he might be missing, he followed at a distance.

Unbeknownst to him, he was the object of complex imaginings on behalf of Cheryl and Tina as they sneaked a peek from the window of the room they shared above the shop, and he was not alone, as the majority of the men in the village had passed thus before their combined scrutiny. These fancies consisted of comparing the imaginings that they had of their male neighbours with the photograph stuck on their bedroom wall of Aidan Turner as *Ross Poldark* in the famous scene from the television series where he scythes his crops, stripped to the waist. Their original version of this picture had been torn from a magazine and unsurprisingly, become grubby, but as that image had become something of an icon of its age, they were able to get hold of more durable copies that would withstand their incessant pawings.

"I don't think that Cyril has any pecs at all" said Cheryl.

"He hasn't got a six-pack- more a chamber pot "

"And as for his lunch box..! "snorted Cheryl.

Downstairs, Henry and Alma smiled contentedly to each other as they heard the shrieks of laughter coming from

above.
Nice to know the girls shared so much.

They were less damning about Jago Hocking. For the most part, they scorned the men of the village. In fact they scorned most men, except for Ross Poldark. But Jago had something of the Ross about him without the television screen between himself and their damp palms. And in the summer, when the sun shone and he went bare-chested down the hill to his boat, they could compare six-packs. When he came in to the shop to buy his copy of 'the Guardian'- the 'Cornish Guardian', that is- and his packets of special cigarette papers, he would look at them in 'that way', say 'Morning ,ladies,' and growl. They tittered dutifully but on more than one occasion,they found that they had actually wet themselves.

Jago was born and bred in the village. Like the other men, he wore light brown leather work-boots, calf-high and steel-toe capped. Not only were they practical but automatically they gave even the feeblest wimp a cowboys swagger. Like the other men, he favoured long, nondescript shorts, either track-suit bottoms cut off below the knee or ancient jeans, similarly curtailed. Nathan and Steve, who had played rugby to a decent level and had had quality kit, wore their old rugby shorts. For the torso, it was either old T-shirts or ancient rugby strips in summer and lumber-jack shirts in winter. While he never favoured a full beard, it was rare to see him clean-shaven. With the Celtic black hair, his four o'clock shadow tended to appear at about half past eleven and his eyes, unless reddened by excess, either of sunshine or less natural stimulants, were ice-blue, making him difficult to typify. He had been taken for a gypsy, often, an Arab, an Albanian and a 'wog' but only the drunken old Brit whom he had come across in India who called him that had any idea what he meant.

Like Laurie Lee, whose books he had read, Jago had set out one midsummer's morning back in late Eighties to see the world. As he stood at the top of the hill, he did not look back because he knew that he probably wouldn't go if he did. Turn left and it was Land's End and the Scilly Isles and he had been there. Turn right, it was Plymouth, London and the rest of the world. No choice.

Jago lived in a squat in Holland Park for a while, until he realised that while London may well have had those pleasures that he had enjoyed in Cornwall and in abundance, it also housed an awful lot of crap, so he made his way to Belgium and the City of Brussels. Here he hung out with the younger, trendier members of the European Parliament , if such a description is not a total impossibility. There was a lot of talk about the future, after the Millennium, in at least three different languages and yet real action seemed hampered by minutiae.

Jago, apparently single-handedly, countered the prevalent flow; thousands of Eastern Europeans were heading for London while he made his way east and south. The beauty and bitterness of Kosovo, the joyous *elan* of the Greeks as they rode headlong into bankruptcy, the tensions of Turkey, the killing fields of the Middle East, be it Gaza, Golan, Iraq or Iran and even once he had made it to Afghanistan where, by now, unacquainted with a barber for several months, he could have been- and was- mistaken for a native,. he could not escape the feeling that what had once been the cradle of civilization had now become its coffin. Although he did not make any conscious effort to dress like a native, his own clothes had gradually needed replacing-his last vestige of underwear had disintegrated just outside Kabul and he wore an interesting fusion that testified, even more clearly than his passport, to his route. He particularly found the pakoul, the flat hat reminiscent in shape at least of a cow pat, particularly comfortable. When he returned, he would wear it instead of the battered peaked cap favoured by the older boatmen or the gaudy baseball hats, worn backwards by the younger men, Sadly it was this hat that had nearly been his downfall.

It was while crossing into Pakistan, high in the Hindu Kush, that a particularly obnoxious border guard, with little English, could not believe Jago's story, or his passport, for that matter, as his hair, beard and clothing were all completely different from the picture of the quite smart-for Jago- young man looking out of the snap. Now, Jago had been warned about guards stealing his money and had read his 'Papillon', Charriere's wonderful book about surviving the Devil Island prison by keeping his valuables

,'where the sun don't shine.' So he had acquired a metal tube, before leaving Cornwall, and kept his return ticket and five 100 dollar travellers' cheques rolled up inside and travelled with it 'in'. True, he had very nearly lost it during one very sudden and violent attack of Chausescu' Revenge (very similar to Montezuma's Revenge but in Romania, the result of a dubious kebab) but quick thinking and a total disregard for where it had landed meant that he had rescued it.

But now, this monstrosity was insisting that he lower his shorts and bend over; he grinned appallingly as he displayed teeth that no dental hygenist had ever cared for and snapped on a single used old Marigold glove, no longer the yellow it once had been. Jago tried to complain in his best British tones ;" I say, this is quite outrageous," but the guard picked up and held a revolver in his other hand. Jago slowly bent forward but just as the man put down the gun, as both hands would have been needed, a voice screamed: "*Rook jar!*!"and Jago saw, looking back over his shoulder, an officer step into the room and without stopping, bringing a cane down on the man's hand and then reverse sweeping it, slashing it across his face twice.

"He is lucky I left my sword at home!"

Majid Khan, it seems, had been for some time at Sandhurst and had fallen in love with most things British; when he learned that Jago was Cornish, he had insisted that he join him in his sparse quarters for a Pakistani army-version of a cream tea, which was, frankly, disgusting. Though the substitute scone was all right, the Lassi, a sort of yoghurt instead of Cornish clotted cream was a disaster and their jam was not strawberry. However, as it was the first solid food that Jago had had for a few days, he was delighted to pretend to enjoy it and Majid's discussion of 'Cornish patsies'- once they had clarified the spelling and pronunciation- made Jago feel quite homesick. For the first time in a very long time, he looked at a world atlas. There was still a long way to go, but an awful lot of it was water.

He trekked the Himalayas, did most of South East Asia by boat on the Mekong River as far as Ho Chi Ming City, learned how to cook a real Thai curry in Bankok, fell in love in and with Bali, until, once they had both realised the impossibility of anything developing, he was ready to go home.

His route was via Sydney where he recognized the inadequacies of Porthwallow as a harbour in comparison but a few weeks' lotus-eating out in the Rocks was enough; after all that sun on Aussie sand, he wanted some good Cornish rain on granite. He came home.

There was commotion up at the White House. Cyril Oliphant had tried to enter the meeting uninvited.

When Lady Olivia, standing at the front door to greet the committee members had asked him who he was, he said: "Oh, I'm with them," indicating Jago and Ashley who had just gone in.

"But what are you doing here?" she asked.

"Well, that was exactly what I was going to ask you. I'm with the local paper."

The Admiral had joined them. "Which one?"

"What?"

"Which paper do you represent?" There are several in Cornwall.

"Well, all of them," said Cyril, blustering." I'm sort of

freelance,and there is obviously something going on that ..er... my readers will want to know about."

"I'm sorry but this is a private party. A beetle drive."

"You're herding insects?!" asked Oliphant, his Adam's apple leaping incredulously.

"Look," said the Admiral," I really think you ought to leave. Bobby!?" He called over his grandson.

"Could you show this person the gate?"

Despite being tall, Cyril was a wimp and Bobby's amateur attempt at a half-Nelson was more than enough to drive him to the gate.

"I only wanted to know what's happening. Nobody ever tells me anything."

"Hardly surprising, if you go about things like that. Good evening. Ah!, evening , Michael!"

He greeted the shadowy figure in the dark hoody that had slipped in as Cyril was being shown out.

"He's involved too?!"thought Cyril. After a sufficient passage of time, during which no-one else had appeared, he slipped back in through the gate and expertly eyed up the ground-floor windows.

Chapter 15

Ashley Pine tapped his gilded biro on his water glass. " Sorry about that slight unpleasantness. Does anyone know him?"

"Incomer from upalong. Been here for a few years now. Dunno if he works, though."said Jago.

"He told me," said Jenny," when he was trying to chat me up, which was one of the most unpleasant experiences of my life, that he had had something to do with GCHQ and that if he told me anymore ,he'd have to kill me, and then himself. I think there was a joke in there somewhere, but I'm not sure where."

"Right," said Ashley," I'd like to call this, the third meeting of the Porthwallow Reconstruction Committee to order. Now, I know there have been various meetings of various sub-committees that have either been charged with or have taken it upon themselves to do something. Which is splendid. But if we 'ave to sit here and listen to all what you've done, we'll be here all night and totally negate the point of sub-committees, so I propose we leave any reports until we've actually done sommat. Right?"

"Seconded," called the Admiral, whose POEMS were in the balance until some of the more wary ones had been persuaded to definitely take part. And until he had been able to find some infallible way of reminding old Mr Collard the difference between his left and his right.

"Can I ask about the PA?" It was Michael.

"Press Association?"

"No-"

"Personal Assistant? I'd be more than willing to volunteer.." offered Jenny, hopefully.

"No. P.A. Public address system. Do you have anything for your carnival- the fete thing?"

"Well, there is something- a microphone and at least one speaker that they set up on the quay..."

"Can't understand a bloody word from it." This from Alf who had been making the same point to the carnival committee for years.

"So we take that as a 'no'?"

"Yes. If you wants to broadcast your band-"

"I think you'll probably hear the band . I was thinking more for announcements.."

"Anything' d be better 'n what we got". said Alf finally.
"I'll have a word. I know some noise boys."
"Now-" Ashley tried to get the meeting going again.
"Us 'as done sommat-"called Jago, from the end of the table.
"Yes, I'm sure we've all noticed the work on the site..."
"No-no that- we'm into re'earsals, in't we ,Vicar?!"
"Yes, I-"
"Rehearsals?!" Jenny Thomas almost screamed. She was having trouble finding a Juliet to play opposite her Nurse, so the news that the men might have made a start was most galling. "What do you lot know about rehearsals?!"
"You says the words often enough 'till you can remember 'em. An'. don't bump in to the furniture- wasn't that what that old poof, Noel Coward- oh, sorry, Vicar- Noel Coward used to say?"
"Yes, but... you haven't got a girl hidden away in your house, have you, Michael?"
Michael was day-dreaming about Sandy, who had something on at school and so couldn't be there.
"What? No- sorry. My house keeper is kept young by Jake

but the grey hair would give it away. She might do Juliet's mum, if you need one. But you'd have to ask her..."

"What about Tegan?" suggested Bobby, offering his current obsession.

"Far too old!"snapped Jenny. "And knowing! She has to be innocent, not...rampant! She'd be telling the Nurse all about how to get laid, not the other way round! "

"Can we get on?" insisted Ashley, displaying his credentials as a chairman. "What about our. .. ah?- 'quintessence'. The merchandise?"

"Well-" said Michael and Jago, both at the same time.

"No, you go ahead," said Jago."I'm sure you're better informed."

"Well,"said Michael," I got my people in London to ..er..ask about and to the best of my knowledge, we could be talking as much as a hundred pounds a gram- although the price might have been hoiked when they found out the sort of people who were asking- I mean, the people from my record company- not you,-er- us- down here."

" Jago?"

"Yeah, well, I agree, I reckon if we work upon a hundred

grand a kilo, it's the sort of money we could well be looking at"
"To pay or to earn?" Lady Olivia was a little confused.
"No, to earn. Ideally."
"Wow!" Alf, the milkman's reaction spoke for all of them.
"That's half a million quid for five kilos. One of those bags of potatoes you sell, Alf. Half a million quid."
" Bloody expensive spuds!"
"And if we are to buy it somewhere overseas," asked the Admiral," what are we going to have to pay at source? That's what we need to know"
"That's the difficult question," said Michael. "We really need someone on the ground to find out."
"Well, I know you're not going to believe this,"said Lady Olivia-" I know I didn't when Sir Cosmo told me but there is actually a de Coverletin our Embassy in Bogota."

Although, within, he knew himself to be a Nissan Qashqai, Philip on the outside looked as though he had been conceived in a fantastical union between Graham Greene and Evelyn Waugh, a cross between 'Our man in

Havana' and William Boot, once arrived in Azania. The sweat-laden linen suit
that once had been white, the crumpled panama, a relic of earlier days on cricket pitches across south east England, even the college tie that he wore at half-mast, all suggested Englishman Abroad.

He smiled to himself as he cruised round the Embassy's corridors; he had received a directive from home."Be prepared for anything." Initially, he had thought that it was yet another of the self-help pamphlets which this new department called HR was sending out which assumed that everyone was miserable and that only its authors, often members of the HR department, had the solution but then he noticed that it was signed 'Cosmo de Courtney'. He admired his cousin and wouldn't not dream of disobeying him, even in something so uncertain, so, with this as his inspiration, he called on the Embassy doctor and asked for: "the works, doc. Full MOT and ten thousand mile service, not forgetting oil and water. Best check the old cam-shaft and clutch while you're down there."

He had then received a very enigmatic follow-up from

Cosmo. "What price half Gradgrind's home town?"
'Gradgrind' had rung a bell with him; somewhere, at some time in the past, beit at school or college under duress or in some lonely, distant embassy library of his own home-sick free will, he had read almost everything Dickens had written, even the other four Christmas stories. 'Hard Times' had not been a favourite but he and Uncle Cosmo had had a discussion about Gradgrind's obsession with fact during one of his previous leaves, and wasn't Coketown a bit obvious for the name of an industrial slum?
" 'Coketown'! He can't mean the 'town' bit-so he must mean 'coke'!. Vrrum! The price of coke? Touch of the old sleuthing called for. Vrrum, vrrum!"

"Is there anything to report from the top of the bill?"
They all looked at Michael, who looked back.
"Have we a date? I hate to be picky but I can't even guarantee a band, let alone ...ah...anything else, until I know when you want us?"
"Haven't we even decided on that?!"snorted Jenny
She was getting hot and bothered. She was afraid it might

be the menopause but was hoping it was simply the others' inefficiency.

"As far as I was aware," replied Ashley, soothing the situation, "there is nothing definite because virtually every day throughout the summer, there's something on somewhere else in Cornwall. I looked at what I could find and was going to suggest the Sunday before August Bank Holiday.

There are lots of things on the actual Monday, not so much the day before. Can we check?"

They all took out their various *aide-memoires*. Alf the milkman had a big old school exercise book wherein he kept his orders and accounts; young Bobby and Ashley had calendars on their smart phones; Jenny an old Filofax , Lady Olivia a tiny diary and silver pen attached by a chain, the Admiral a big black Letts desk diary while the Vicar carried something provided by the Church of England. The others looked at their neighbours'.

"Bank Holiday is Polruan Regatta, always has been." said Jago.

"But we shouldn't clash with anything they do. Offer any

similar attractions?"

"No, but if the locals get pissed up with us watching Michael here on the Sunday, it could seriously affect the takings next day downalong."

"I don't really think we can allow such considerations..." said Ashley

"But it might stop some of they good old boys comin' to us," said Jago

"If the prospect of getting drunk on Monday is going to stop people coming to see one of the greatest rock bands in the world, then I wonder, do we really want them!?"

"Well said, Vicar" said the Admiral.

"My", said Michael, "No pressure then. "

"Do you think you can get your band together for then?"

" Probably but I can't promise. But no publicity until I know for sure. Agreed?"

When the rest of the committee heard the edge on Michael's usually softly-spoken whisper, they began to understand how he had had the steel to make it to the top and stay there ever since. Cyril Oliphant smiled to himself as he withdrew his ear from the window and he crept out of the garden.

MICHAEL AND THE ANGELS TO PLAY AT PORTHWALLOW.

None of the reputable papers had dared print the whisper that had been left on their ansaphones; it was only one of the freebees, the MidCornwall Gazette, whose editor was glad of any information at all, that had dared carry the headline. He felt rather smug, having scooped everybody.

That was until the day after weekly publication when a very smart Daimler pulled into the yard outside the building that he shared with the rest of the rags and two smooth gentlemen in very expensive suits asked for him. They subsequently asked for the name of his source and when he pompously denied on the grounds of the right of the Press to protect their sources, one carefully poured half a cup of coffee over the open laptop in front of the man. With the cup poised over the desk-top computer, which contained the data for the entire publication, he asked the question again, including a request for the telephone number as well..

"I dunno his whole name but the surname is Oliphant- lives in the wretched village, he says. Has got loads more stories, he says." But the men had gone.

Cyril answered the knock on his stable-style door, opening the top half. The two men in dark glasses looked so out of place in Porthwallow..

"Yes?"

"Mr. Cyril Oliphant?"

"Yes."

"Is this your phone number?" The man recited is number correctly.

"Yes."

"Do you happen to have your phone with you?"

As he replied, "Yes. Look, what is this? Have I won something? I did go in for that holiday on the telly..." he handed it over and could not believe his eyes as the other man, who had not spoken, reached out for the phone which Cyril always had with him. He didn't want to miss a thing.

What he hadn't noticed was the stylish wooden-handled ice-pick usually used for chipping ice in high-class cocktail lounges that seemed to appear from nowhere but in fact had been couched up the man's sleeve. He didn't miss the fact that the man with the pick then buried it in Cyril's expensive android several times. He then returned the wreck to him.

"Next time," said the first," it will be your hand. Then, if really necessarily, your head. Missing you already."

They then got into the saloon and drove quietly away.

"This is Michael,"

"A voice from the nether world!" replied Andy, 'Saint Andrew' and lead guitarist with the band.

"Cornwall is not that far away, as you'd know if only you came down and visited your godson!"

"How is Jake?"

"Loving it."

"And his father?"

It took Michael a little longer to reply.

"Great. No, really great. Much better. Are you ready?"

"Am I ready? I've been ready since the O 2."

Michael explained the event.

"Love it. LOVE IT. So where do we rehearse? Not down

your way, it'd be a give-away. Even if we went back to the Sawmills, people would soon get to know."

"You could always come down and see the boy. And his father"

Which is how the rumour got about the village that the greatest rock guitarist since Eric Clapton had been seen up at Michael's place. When the two of them, Michael and Andy, walked into the pub, the place went deadly silent for a second, the eyes of all those there flicked about the room, straight out of every B-Western, checking with their friends and drinking companions- not always the same- that what they had just seen was true, and then things went on as before, except possibly a notch or two higher in volume.

"Is Roger there?" Michael did not recognise the young woman's voice but was pretty sure it was the right number.

"I'll check. Who shall I say is calling?"

"My name is Michael Donovan."

"Mikey! Uncle Mikey! Oh my God, like wow, like I so don't believe it's you!"

"Excuse me but who is this?"

"Uncle Mikeee-like, who do you think it might be answering my dad's phone?!"
"Katie?"
"'Catherine', please. I'm fourteen. No-one over twelve is called Katie, except that... Mrs Andre! Dad, you'll never guess?"She was obviously talking to someone away from her now.
"Only THE Michael Donovan!" The sound of a struggle for the 'phone and then a man's voice:
"Michael?! How the devil are you? More to the point,where are you and when are we going to see you? Catherine, will you let go!"
So the appointment for Michael to go to visit the Cross family, uncle Gary included ,was made and the brothers were even more on board than Andy, if such a thing were possible.
"D'you think Abbey Road would be free?" Michael asked.
"That'll be the day- Abbey Road, free!"
"You know what I mean, 'available'"
"I'll get our people to find out -if we still have 'people'."
"And no whispers. Not even to Catherine! Especially

Catherine. Don't tell her yet. And I'm really serious. I believe the last blabbermouth actually wets himself every time there is a knock on his front door these days."

Chapter 16

The Mechanicals, as the workmen of the village, plus the Vicar, who said that he qualified as a labourer in Life's vineyard., called themselves were facing a problem. Nathan was having difficulties pitching his voice high.

"Makes me sound a right arse- sorry, Vicar."

"But that's the whole point-,"replied the Vicar, "It is comic- farcical, even."

"An' anyway, I can't do it."

"Imagine," said Jago, " I dunno, imagine some ugly bastard- sorry, Vicar- like 'H' here 'as got hold of your balls- sorry, Vicar!"

"No, no- that's quite all right. After all, we all...eh "He cleared his throat." Have ah- balls!" He was enjoying the new sensation of being part of such a masculine ensemble.

"Right, he's got yer balls at the bottom of a scrum and is twistin'?"

"Ah, we got sommat special fer that, in'us, Steve? Anything right dirty and we 'as a call. *Onnen hag oll,* inn'it, Steve? One and all!"

The farmer nodded his head and continued: "That's it- the

old Cornish motto-then it's all onter the one. No referee can 'andle it and the dirty bugger- sorry, Vicar- 'e'll never try it again- that is, if 'e can walk."

"Trouble is,"Jago tried to explain," if you says it normal- what's the line?"

Nathan replied deadpan: "

Most radiant Pyramus, most lily-white of hue,
Of colour like the red rose on triumphant brier,
Most brisky juvenal and eke most lovely Jew,
As true as truest horse that yet would never tire,"

"See?" said Jago," Not a titter; but if you imagine you got yer nadgers in a trap- "And here he raised his voice three full octaves:

"Most radiant Pyramus" the others were all laughing before he had finished the first line.

"Well, you play the fuckin' part" said Nathan. "Sorry, Vicar! An' there's something else I don't understand"

"Just the one?" asked H.

"No but, why does Jay come back on with a donkey's 'ead on? An' is there gonna be some poor donkey up the sanctuary walkin' around without a 'ead on?"

"Naw," said Jago ,"Tis bein' made up Lunnon. Mates of Mike, I s'ppose cos they'm called 'Angels' as well. "
"But why a donkey?"
"Well, what sort of bloke is 'e, this Bottom? "
"Well, Bottom- tha's just a polite name fer 'arse' fer a start- "said Nathan, " So-A right, Dick'ead!"
"Exactly,!" said the Vicar," But they couldn't have him wearing...one of those on his head, even back then, so they had Bottom wear a donkey- or ass's head!"

Rehearsals for the scenes from Shakespeare were varied, very varied. Mrs Guthrie, who had asked Jenny to call her 'Rosemary' was happy to play Lady Capulet and was discovered to be very good.
"You've done this before," said Jenny, a mixture of gratitude and envy in her voice.
"Twenty years, on and off- more off than on, like most actors, until I decided that admitting defeat was preferable to starvation. I've been a house-keeper stroke nanny for nearly twenty years now- seven with Michael, and as you can see, have more than made up for the hunger years."

"You'll have to help with Juliet, then."

"I'd love to- who have you got?"

"Well-"

And Jenny described her search for someone local who could be believable both as a fourteen-year old and a virgin.

"Not easy".

She had done the obvious: and tried the local secondary school.

The local school has changed its name more often than the musician formerly known as Prince.

After it had been closed as the local grammar school, what was left, at least to begin with, was known as the South East Cornwall Secondary School, until a bright student put the initials together and it was known as the SECS School which wasn't far from the truth.

It then became a college following the directive from the Department of Education (which was undecided as to whether it was 'for' or 'of"; it too changed its name often, the most amusing one being the Department for Children, Schools and Families, with no mention of Education) and when that change of name made little difference -(the bright ones still did quite well and the others couldn't give a toss-) they tried again and the latest name on the board outside is the South East Cornwall Academy. What used to be the sports hall is now 'the Sports Hub'.

Jenny rang and mentioned the festival and so was given an appointment to see the Head Master.

The school girl who had answered the phone had replied: "The Boss? No worries, mate".

Jenny had put on something a bit smart; after all, it was the Head Master but when she got there, she realised that she might not have bothered.

The man who came to see her, hand outstretched was dressed in a pink polo shirt under a smart lime-coloured tracksuit with the logo :'SECA' emblazoned on his chest.

"Hi, I'm Tim," he had said and then something which sounded like: 'See you'.

"Goodbye?"

"No, C.E.O! I'm the Chief Executive. The Boss." There was an accent there

"Is that the same as Head Master?" Jenny was bemused.

"Oh, listen- no way. We've done away with all that. Same as sex." Australian! It came out 'sacks'.

"What?!"

"All that confusion between 'sex' and 'gender'?" The infernal intonation!

"I don't think we go in for gender on Porthwallow. The other, yes!" It was always worth a try.

"Listen, Jenny. Is it all right if I call you 'Jenny'?" He went on without waiting for an answer. "You want to see our drama supremo, Cheyanne. Hey," he called to a passing girl, "Mave, show this lady to the drama cube, will ya?"

"Sir,"

"Listen, I told you, at that voluntary assembly you all missed, it's ' Tim' on campus."

"Yessir- I were'nt sure what 'campus' meant"

"Aren't they so lovely?!- you just want to squeeze them - by the throat!" And he playfully throttled the girl, who chanted: "Oh eight hundred one one one one." Tim let go as if electrocuted.

"The drama cube, now! Nice to met you." And he hurried off down the corridor.

"Your headmaster?"

"He's a wanka, miss."

"What was that magic number?"

"Childline, miss. These days, kids learn that sooner n' they can say 'dada'. Sometimes, instead of it."

"Oh, and what about the drama here?"

" Bunch a wankas. Load a gays n' drama queens, even the blokes."

"Are you in the school play?"

"Play?! Nah- More's the pi'y. Don't do plays no more."

As they walked along the corridor, they could hear, getting ever louder, the beat of Eminem's 'Rap God'. They reached a door at the end; Mavis opened it, inclined her head to indicate to Jenny to enter and then shut the door behind her.

It could have been taken for a twenty-first century version of Hieronymus Bosch's "Garden of Earthly Delights."

A dozen or more portly teenage girls, none of whom had obviously seen themselves from behind in black lycra, black T-shirts, died black hair, tied up in a topknot so they looked like unfit sumo wrestlers, and giant panda-style eye make-up, currently all barefoot although a pile of black Doc.Marten boots at the side showed that their taste in footwear was as universal as for everything else, each clutching a bare broom handle, gyrated individually while a very basic sound-to-light system in turn illuminated a few garish spot lights. Two boys, this time stick-insect-thin with absolutely no buttocks to keep their black Levis' up and diagonal fringes long enough to hide behind , stuck together.

Coming out of this crowd toward Jenny was Cheyanne, a confusing figure: chubby would have been polite; died white hair cut shaggy-short, a primitive make-up consisting of white pan-cake, pencil-thin horizontal black eye brows well above her natural brow and cherry red lipstick, hi-viz pink t-shirt, a very obvious absence of brassiere, baggy old stone-washed blue denim bib-and- braces overalls, fashionably ripped at the knees, red baseball boots,   but most remarkable, eight or nine charity-support ribbons all over her chest.

Along with the common ones to start, inevitably, the rainbow one, then the red for AIDS, the pink for Breast

Cancer, white for Blindness, blue for Arthritis, there were really rare ones: black for Sleep Apnea, brown for colon cancer, burgundy for meningitis, and green for Bipolar and depression. Jenny had an awful thought for a moment about whether Cheyanne and her friends sat round in circles and swapped those they didn't have already but quickly tried to dismiss it..

"Yes?"yelled the other.

Jenny tried to introduce herself but failed dismally when up against Marshall Mathers.

"Lionel?!," she yelled and when one of the boys detached himself from the crush, signalled for him to turn the music down.

When she could hear herself speak, she said ; "Hey, dudes. Chill." The students sat on the floor and said and did nothing.

"Hi, I'm Cheyanne."

Jenny had to struggle briefly to keep a straight face but soon explained the festival, her search for an actress- although, looking at the girls on display here, rather hoped that none would put herself forward.

Fortunately, Cheyanne saved any embarrassment.

"Like, Jen- me and the crew, we don' do your actual actin'. Our bag is Drama. It's, like, Drama GCSE and tha' is all down to the communi'y." Fashionably, she seemed to abhor most 't's.

"Come togever, knaw wha' ah mean?" Cheyanne was obviously not of West Indian origin but apparently favoured their phraseology.

"Well, would you and your...'crew' like to come and perform at the festival?"

"Like....I mean, knaw wha' I mean- 'perform'? We don't dig 'perform'- i' is.. hierarchical- We maintain the class struggle against the phallocra' ic socie-y. - vem an' us, knaw wha ah mean?"

"Well, don't let me keep you, but if you change your mind, you'll probably be on just before Michael and the Angels"

This shattered Cheyanne's whole persona. Somehow the diction neared Cheslea.

"Not really?!?Wow? Oh, my God! I mean, hey, guys, guys, listen in- we could be giggin' with Michael and the Angels! Like, how cool is that?!"

Jenny slipped out, leaving uproar in the Cube, which seemed to be more of an oblong like most classrooms and only slightly noisier..

Mavis was still waiting outside.

"Shouldn't you be in lessons?"

"Oh, Tim doesn't mind. If we have a personal crisis, we just go to our councillor. But I was going to ask, do you need someone to actually act, not ...piss about to Cheyanne's favourite music?"

Jenny looked at her.

"You want to try?"

"More than anything else in the world."

Spring had definitely taken hold, The hedgerows beside the narrow Cornish lanes had begun their ceaseless, wondrous round of change, from snowdrops to primroses with the promise of the bluebells, campion and wild garlic and the blossoms on the thorns to come. The gorse was golden and the celandine almost metallic in their yellow .

"Come on," said Tegan, playfully dragging young Bobby up the path to the woods and the hills beyond. To anyone who, like Bobby, had skied since childhood from the family chalet in Verbier, to call the sloping woodland up the coombe 'hills' was ludicrous but the path did incline upwards for a breath-shortening distance and then undulated satisfactorily round a pill, past the one-time haunt of druids, the holy well of old St Wallow's-, now contained in what could fancifully have been a stone sarcophagus but in all likelihood is simply an ancient drinking trough for cows before it trickled down to eventually join the sea. No need for waterproofs, it was woolies and 'wellies', although after the climb they had both taken off their sweaters with Tegan hanging hers round her neck and Bobby tying his round his waist.

They sat on an old wooden bench, its colour no longer discernible. This parcel of land was not yet owned by the National Trust and so had not been subjected to their treatment: neat oak styles, bearing cleanly carved coloured directional arrows, chunky pine risers for the steps all held in place by burly metal claws and benches which more often than not had been refurbished or dedicated to particularly generous local benefactors.

Bobby reached for Tegan's mouth with his and her breast with a hand, which she slapped.

"No! There is a time and a place for everything. Just look about you. Not even I, in all my splendour, can match all this."

So they sat there , fingers intertwined. and discussed dog violets, though neither of their minds was really on the subject. Sadly, both the young people had allowed themselves to succumb to the dreadful, prevalent fad for tattoos. Time was when 'love' and 'hate' across one's knuckles and possibly an anchor on the biceps were the depths to which some exhibitionists would sink. But recently these illustrations had reached epidemic proportions and Bobby's forearm looked as though it were a putrescent boa constrictor and his calves were little better. Tegan, at least, had some self-awareness, and so her lines, all black , looked like a geometric puzzle conceived by a lunatic Maori.

"So," asked Tegan," What has Dame Judi got you doing?"

"Who?"

"Jenny. Porthwallow's answer to RADA's finest?" Bobby had come to realise the competition, almost the antagonism between the two women.
"Oh. She says I'm too old to play Romeo."
"What she means is she'd too old to play Juliet."
"Yeah, well...said I couldn't begin to handle Hamlet."
"Because she thinks she's too old for Ophelia, and it's not much of a part anyway, and Gertrude would be admitting that you could be her son."
"Which is more than possible, isn't it? I mean, her boy Jim must be nearly thirty, isn't he? "
And then a voice from the trees behind said:
"Ah, but you don't never discuss a lady's age, specially if that lady's our Jen!"
"Who the hell...?" Bobby leapt to his feet, his hopes that Tegan might change her mind momentarily dashed.
"Uncle Jack!" She swivelled on the bench and looked into the bush. "You didn't ought to creep up and people like that- you might see things you wasn't supposed to!"
"Never knows me luck. Don't think we've met, Master 'Awkins. Jack Paynter. I lives...

"Ah," said Bobby, collecting himself."Yes! 'The Man who Lives in the Woods."

"And who don't shit in the old pigsty!"

"How did you...!"

"Ah- less said, soonest mended."

Bobby looked at the old man. Everything was brown, from the knitted woollen hat to even ,somehow, the Wellington boots, a mixture of mahogany-coloured skin where visible, mackintosh, vest, army-surplus shirt and ancient, cavalry-twill trousers. And broad leather belt. He looked at the ground all the while that he spoke.

"Tell 'ee what, now that I've seen 'ee- taller than the old Admiral, in't yer? Yes.- I'd say...Ferdinand in 'the Tempest' or Benedict in 'Much Ado.' Then our Jen can play 'Beatrice'.. Can't stop. Give my best to your mother, maid"

And he shuffled shyly off up into the woods.

"So that is the -?"

And Tegan joined him:"Man who Lives in the Woods." I was hoping we might tempt him out."

"Was I the bait? Or you?"

"Both."

"How comes he knows his Shakespeare?"

"He hasn't always lived in the woods. He went to London. Got a job at the Aldwych Theatre as a stage hand and when the RSC moved...."

"Who?

"Royal Shakespeare Company, philistine! They were based there in London and when they moved, he stayed with them but went to HQ in Stratford. You've heard of Stratford?!"

"All right, all right!"

"Well, and then - I know it's hard to believe- but they do say he was a flyman at Stratford- watched every performance of almost all old Bill's plays, but from the fly gallery. Above the stage. Can recognise the entire acting profession by the tops of their heads. But he retired, maybe twenty years ago and while he had been away, it was all change. That was when the second-homers started looking for places to buy . Uncle Jack was one of six was raised by his mum and dad in one of those two-up-two downs along the shore. Father had died and the other children moved away so when his mum was offered thirty grand and one of the new one-bed council bungalows they'd just built at the top of the hill, she didn't think. She jumped at it. Worth two hundred grand now. Only thing was, there wasn't any room for Uncle Jack. So he built this place out here somewhere- I don't know where. No-one has ever seen it. And the Man who Lives in the Woods has been here ever since. Sometimes really famous actors, old ones I've actually seen on telly will come down on holiday and Uncle Jack will have a real piss-up with them for old times' sakes in the pub."

Chapter 17

"How much?"

Lady Olivia asked old Pete, the ancient taxi driver and mechanic. Although he had officially retired twenty years earlier, he still kept up a steady trade with the older villagers as their visits to hospital in Treliske had increased.

"Um...five pound, milady," he growled.

"Oh, don't be ridiculous! The ferry tickets alone will have cost twice that! Where on earth did you get such a ludicrous figure from?"

"Waal, I reckon twas about that last time us went down Truro together."

"But I haven't been to hospital for about fifty years! "

"Reckon! How d'you spect me to keep body an' soul together if you only uses we ev'ry fifty year!"

"Oh, you are a ridiculous man! Here's fifty. And if you argue, I shall send for a taxi from Looe next time!"

"Yes, ma-am."

"And no mention of this, please, Pete."

"No, mum,"

"I know all about the Porthwallow grapevine. They know

you're back before your bottom hits the chair."

"Course not, mum. My lips is sealed"

Which was how the whole village-or at least, those who knew and cared for her- learned that lady Olivia Vincent had pancreatic cancer.

When Sir Robert and Michael were finally summoned, they knew but had to pretend that they didn't. The Vicar had already been to see her and was already trying to practise those terrible words of the funeral service. "In the midst of life..."without a lump in his throat.

"Well, my dears, let's not beat about the bush. Eighty seven is a pretty good innings but it looks as thought some bloody cancer-thing had got me stumped. I didn't even know I had a pancreas- thought it was that silly station you have to get to if you want to catch the Eurostar."

"But you can't," said the Admiral," I need you as reserve in the Mobility display team."

"Another pleasure I shall have to miss. I shan't mind not making it to one hundred- I've more than enough little notes and things, thank-you letters and what have you from dear Lillibet without wanting a mass-produced telegram that's supposed to be from her. If she is still with us, of course- it could be Big Ears. No, but I shall mind missing all the fun with the festival and you, dear-"Here she nodded to Michael, "you playing with all your wonderfully talented friends. So I'm going to be awfully devious and count upon you agreeing to almost anything some decrepit old fool might ask ."

"Oh, Lady Olivia-"Michael started to reply but she interrupted.

"Call me 'Olive,' dear-like Bobby does. So much more homely- less ...'up' oneself, don't you think?"

"Olive, if I can, I'll do it."

"I want you to sing for me. At my...do. Funeral...thing. I think bits of me'll still be somewhere about, even if I'm not in that actual, awful box...please?"

The old lady maintained her habitual lightness as well as she could but every now and then the dark shadow could be seen lurking.

"Of course."

"And don't go naming the bloody place after me- it is to be the Porthwallow Village Hall." There was a pause as the two men could think of nothing appropriate to say.

"Have I told you lately that I love you"

"What?" Both men started.

"What I want you to sing. You do know it, I hope?"

"Oh, yes," said Michael, once he had recovered from his misunderstanding. "I even know Van Morrison a bit. A unique voice."

"Well, actually, I was thinking of what's his name-'Do you think I'm sexy" That's a quote not a question- Rob? Rod?"

"Stewart."

"Yes, Rod Stewart- do you know him,too?"

"Well, he spends much of his time in LA, but yes, I have met him too- you do, back stage at some of these charity gigs."

"Well, if you can sound anything like him, darling, I shall be more than pleased. But I'm tired"

The two men got up to go but she went on.

"Bobby, would you mind- I'd like a little word."

It was really very quick. Once Lady Olivia decided to do something , she got on with it, and as in life, so in death.

The family doctor kept her out of pain but she only lasted a week.

The old church up the coombe was packed. Not many of the family in the first few pews; there were so few left; from Mean Dhu, only young Sir Cosmo, his immaculate dress suit covering his 'Let It Bleed' T-shirt and Hives, with tears pouring down his face throughout the service. There were one or two cousins and nephews and nieces from Town but so few of them had ever bothered to come down and visit before. Most didn't realise that she had been still alive. And now it was too late.

But the rest of the place was packed. Anyone who felt that they were part of the village got out their best Births, Deaths and Marriages suits, ironed a black tie or found a black frock and prepared to say good bye. Many had never seen the old lady but all knew of her. They never called the White House by that name, it was always 'Lady Olivia's' and she had often been seen, drinking tea on the patio with the sea grumbling two hundred feet below. True, there were now some who had been sent to live in the village by the Council, one step away from an ASBO; they didn't want to be there, but as long as they got what they believed to be their due, their white cider and a 48inch plasma screen, they did little. Everybody else packed the beautiful old place. Even the Man who Lives in the Woods was there, standing among the local men at the back and even he had found a shirt that was grey with age, with a collar that was blue and a black tie from somewhere.

Trevor hated taking funerals; he wasn't sure if he really believed in everything that he was promising. Resurrection had always been a stumbling block. The only thing he did feel sure about at this service was when he said:" Blessed are they that mourn, for they shall be comforted. "

There was an animal sound, almost like cattle, as everybody there agreed. The comforting was mutual, tangible. Trevor didn't even try to eulogize. He left that to the old Admiral. There in full dress uniform plus medals, Sir Robert marched as well he could to the lectern, took out his notes, looked at them, tore them in half and put them back in his pocket.

"I loved Olivia Bolitho all my life . Sorry, family- of course, I loved your Grand-mama but even she knew that she was second best. After Olive. Sadly Olive had fallen in love elsewhere. Here -with the White House- far preferable than a tiny cabin at the Britannia Royal Naval College just after the War- and as it belonged to Nick Vincent's family,- Sir Nicholas Vincent- marrying him was a price that she was prepared to pay to live there and she graced it for nearly seventy years. I bought the' Crow's Nest' to be near her. But it wasn't the same." He glanced at the coffin and the little portrait photograph standing on it in the middle of the wreath.

" We all know that when her Isaac died on Tumbledown, that what the Frogs call her '*raison d'etre*'- curious, really- we Brits don't have a good word for that, do we?-her reason for being really died with him. Nick didn't last much longer and for more than thirty years, she has had the White House to herself. Now, she has left it. Or has she?" And he nodded to Michael who was standing on the other side of the nave.

A single note was played on the organ.

" 'Have I told you lately that I love you?'"

The unique voice rang round the ribs of the church roof.

"'Have I told you there's no one else above you?"

But then Michael suddenly saw a vision of his dead wife, Joanna, looking coolly and smiling at him across the whole congregation. He coughed and went on.

"Fill my heart with gladness." But when he got to he next line, he could go no further. There was a shuffling and a sniffling in the people

"Take away... take away..."And then he muttered :"My sadness.".And then he felt a presence by his side and a little hand in his. He looked down at Jake, who had slipped out from beside Mrs Guthrie and come to join him.

"D'you see Mummy too?" the boy whispered with a smile and then the clear treble sang quietly.

"Ease my troubles. that's what you do." It was enough to get him back on track and by the time father and son had reached :"And at the end of the day-"everyone had joined them and was singing through their tears:"

" We should give thanks and pray
To the one, to the one"

The retiring collection, announced as to be going toward the rebuilding of the hall, was the biggest that they had ever had, beating even the Millennium Midnight Mass. It included a whole wad of fifty pound notes, bound together with a thick pink elastic band. They had more than a thousand pound already, for when funds were needed.

During the wake in the pub after, Ashley Pine stood with his back to the bar, a large vodka and tonic in his pudgy hand. "Dunno 'ow 'e did that, but by 'eck, that were summat.!"

Then the unwelcome face of Cyril Oliphant, body attached, came into the crowded bar. He had decided that this would be a good time to make an appearance. People took one look and the throng parted, reminiscent of the Red Sea, especially when they recognised his companion.

"Ah" called Jago, his fourth pint of Guinness disappearing fast. Jago drank very rarely in the day time but when he did, he tended to make up for irregularity with excess. "Turd of the Yard."

"Now, there's no need to be offensive or I'll be round here tonight checking for lock-ins."

It was, indeed, Inspector Foot.

Cyril had reported the attack on his phone at the time.. He

had been given a crime number and told that, in the absence of any CCTV evidence or an eye-witness version of the actual crime taking place, the police could do little about it. Seeing the announcement of Lady Olivia's funeral in the Western Morning News, Inspector Foot had decided to kill two birds; follow up the complaint about the 'phone and that nagging memory of the smell, permeating the village.
"I wan't being rude, Inspector- You'm Mr Foot. An' everyone knaws, a foot is a third of a yard!" His cronies brayed.

Foot should have known better but didn't.
"Ah, but you said..." And here he lowered his voice. "'Turd'"
"Ah, that's just my impediment. You'll not be knocking an impediment, surely? I can't say' third'- have to say 'turd!"
"But you just did.! You did! You said 'third.' clearly, not 'turd'/"
"Ah, but I wasn't referring to you, Mr Foot. It was meant for your friend." And he turned his back on the two of them.

"You see how it is?" said Oliphant, his Adam's apple

fluctuating and his glasses glinting petulantly.

"Do you want to press charges?"

"What charges could I press?"

"Depends on what the people here have done. To you."

"Well, it wasn't to me actually and not by anyone here. I didn't recognise them."

Jago and Nathan pushed past them, heading for the outside area where inveterate smokers were allowed to indulge their filthy habit.

"Well," said Oliphant, hopefully." Shall we have a drink, now that we're here?"

"Not for me, thank you, not while I'm on duty but don't let me stop you."

"Oh," said Oliphant, " In that case- I was hoping you- but...no.. We might as well go."

Outside, Foot was stopped in his tracks.

"There it is again-that smell?"

"Capstan Full Strength!" Jago called out to the two men.

"Ah, I see...." His mind temporarily at rest, Inspector Foot concentrated on the impression he was intending to make upon the few people that might see him.

Michael couldn't face the wake and asked Sandy if she'd like to have a cup of tea

"There's one thing I don't understand," It was Alf the milkman, a wonderfully reliable soul; if it was humanly possible for a man to fight his way to your door of a morning, then the milk would get through. And he billed monthly, which helped a lot of the pensioners. He had been coerced into taking the part of Starveling, who portrayed the Moon in the play. He had a slow way of speaking which belied a quick brain but which made him an easy butt to his friends .

"Just the one?" asked Jago.

"No, but you'm right there; p'raps I should of said 'several'."

This grammatical flaw, unknowingly replacing the auxiliary verb 'have' with a preposition of all things, had reached pandemic proportions and not only in the village. It niggled the pedant in the Vicar no end who was sure his tutors at Oxford would be steadily revolving in their graves, those that had not been cremated at Headington.

However, this was not the place, among these chaps

labouring so manfully for such good reasons, to pick them up.

"Anyway," said Alf, " what I wants to know is why does the moon 'ave ter speak? Can't I just shine?"

"You obviously 'aven't read yer lines." said Jago.

"And that's another thing- lines! Nobody didn't say nothing about lines. Whole point about the moon-the man in the moon, 'ee don't say nothing."

"But look," said H who, now that he had mastered the really rather complicated and theatrically advanced concept of a man playing a wall, "this in't real life , not what we calls your actual realism, we'm -what's the word, Vicar? 'Ally something?""

"'Allegorical?'"

"Tha's 'ee! Shows the benefit of 'aving the Vicar on board!"

But Jago was getting annoyed.

"But the bleddy moon don't 'ave ter say bugger all!-sorry , Vicar. All you has ter do is stand there holding a lantern, a dog- your mutt will do, long as 'e be'aves hisself- and a thorn bush. Though why...?"He looked at the Vicar; this all reminded Trevor of his years of teaching. And he of all of them was the only one with a fully-annotated text, appropriated during his former career; the others only had copies of their pages which Jeremy had printed off the computer - and who was acquainted with wonders of footnotes. He quickly glanced at the back and explained: "It seems that carrying the thorn bush represented the forest and the lantern shining through was the moon shining through the trees."

"Fuck me- sorry, Vicar," said H "but, like I said, 'elps 'avin' God on yer side!"

They continued the discussion in the pub after.

"What you 'avin', Vicar-"

"Oh, do call me 'Trevor."

"Right, Trev. what is it-' vod and ton' usually, isn't it?"asked Jago.

"Yes, but you know, I'd really rather like some cider- do you sell local cider?" he asked Charlie, the publican who was serving them himself.

"Yeah, but-"

"But me no buts! That might be Shakespeare, I'm not sure

but no, I really want to try some. I've been in this wretched place - no, I don't mean that at all- 'lovely' place for twenty years and never had the real thing."

"If you insist, Vicar-" said Charlie

"Trevor!"

"Trevor, but be careful.!"

Sadly, the cider was so good and the company so convivial that he discovered, an hour later, as he tried to stand up that his legs would no longer obey him, and Steve the farmer had to drive him home, riding pillion on the back of his quad bike. Jeremy was not impressed.

Chapter 18

"I'd like to bring the fourth meeting of the Porthwallow Village Hall Committee to order. "

It was Ashley again.

There was very little disorder for him to control. They all sat around the dining table at the White House, each in the seat that they had adopted as their own but the chair at the foot seemed very empty.

"We can't just wade in without marking Lady Olivia's...er..passing. Vicar, d'you want to say a few words?"

"I've already said my bit. More than"

"Admiral?"

"Me too." The old sailor was looking as though he had aged ten years in the past month and was beginning to appear his real age.

"Anybody?"

After a pause, Alf the milkman, who was a stalwart supporter of Plymouth Argyle, spoke up.

" Just recent, we've taken to a minute's applause before the game, when ever any of they old stars 'as passed, or we jus' wants to show- wossname?"

"Solidarity?" offered Jago.

"That's the word- solidarity. And respect. Tis just an idea?"

Jenny said, as kindly as she could manage,:"I don't think we could produce thunderous applause. Not compared with a football crowd. Not even one the size that turn up at Argyle these days."

"It was just an idea."

"What about the old minute's silence? We could even hold hands."suggested Michael, seated next to Sandy.

"It's not a bloody seance," growled the Admiral.

"Just the minute's silence, then." said the Vicar. " Jeremy, will you be our time-keeper? And put something in the minutes?"

"Of course."

It was impeccably observed , the only sound being the sniffling from Dorothy Dingle, out of sight in the corridor. She was being retained at the moment and did not lose a chance to display how upset she was to anyone who might influence her eventual remittance.

"Thank you," said Jeremy, looking at his watch.

"So," said Ashley." Sub-committee reports?"

"Well," said Michael," If Bobby could just check the windows for eavesdroppers- though I doubt that bastard'll be back- sorry, Vicar. "

The young man did as he was asked.

" Then I think I can announce that Michael and the Angels are happy to play at the 'event.' Very happy"

The air of excitement was palpable; they had all been so 'down' after Lady Olivia's death that no-one had been prepared to ask.

"And ," said the Admiral, caught between the twin emotions of sorrow for the occasion and pleasure for his news."I have another piece of news which might just fill in one of the many gaps in our plan."

This hiked the expectation even further.

"I have just had a communication." He took a very official slip of paper-" I can't be doing with emails and Twits-"

"Tweets, Granmps." said Bobby, smiling in embarrassment.

"Whatever! I like chitties-"And he read: " HMS Runcorn" and stopped again- " Anybody notice anything?"

"That's Jim's boat!" cried Jenny.

" 'Ship', madame, ship! Even if it is no bigger than a tin of pilchards, they are still 'ships' .Only submarines can be called 'boats'!

"Oh, pardon me for living!"

" If I called your wings 'flies' or your tabs 'curtains', you'd be miffed..?"

"Sorry."

"As Jenny so rightly observed, HMS Runcorn just so happens to be the ship her boy is on. She has been ordered to Cartagena- which as you all know, is Colombia's naval base- for a courtesy visit. She will be patrolling the Caribbean for a few weeks and end up being shown a good time by the Colombian navy. That last bit is my own. HMS Mersey was supposed to be going but I've still got a few tentacles wriggling round the old M o D. and a word or two in the right ears, most of which I've boxed in my time, managed to get that changed. Present Lord used to be my 'snotty' on 'Bulwark'-It all helps! Haven't told your boy anything, except to stock up on the old sunblock."

The back streets of Bogota were not Philip's natural stamping grounds. Or 'race tracks' as he liked to think of them.

"Unlikely to get a chance to even get out of third gear! Not to mention sixth gear, manual shift, four wheel drive mode!" But that was where he knew he would have to go.

He had begun his covert operations in the British Embassy; he himself felt pretty immune in the building and so wasn't too worried about keeping his voice down in the canteen.

"Anyone actually know how to actually get hold of this stuff? And any idea what it'd going to cost? Does it have to be US dollars or d'you reckon they'd take travellers' checks, what?"

All the locals kept their faces as stony and motionless as those of the Inca gods outside and denied that they even understood the questions, let alone the answers. After a few days, Philip stopped asking his questions, only to be summoned into the presence of his boss, H.E.

"Second gear, indicate, foot brake, hand brake, switch off." he muttered to himself as he entered the office. "Your Excellency?"

"Ah, Philip-no, don't bother sitting, this won't take long-it's just that I've been getting some rather worrying whispers that you might be buying....ah.....cocaine? This cannot be true, surely?"

"Absolutely...not! I'm after info, not the old Peruvian marching powder itself. I've got a chum, you'll probably have heard of him, writes books, you read books- wants to get his details right, can't stand the heat out here-or afford the fare , if we're to be quite honest -no money in writing, it seems- anyway, after a spot of info and, well...I'm going to let him have it. Okay, yah?"

The Ambassador was a recent appointment and of that class that used such language.

"Ah...yah! Right- fine..er..carry on!"

"Ignition, check the mirrors, indicate and manoeuvre."

It was a great benefit being considered loopy by one's boss.

But when he had returned to the cubby-hole that was called his office and which he had to share with the cultural *attache,* he found a grubby piece of paper on top of all the other grubby pieces of paper on his desk. It simply read :

1g= $3.50

"Hah!" Philip said, loudly, wanting to be heard. "Very interesting!"

"What is?" asked the Cultural *Attache,* idly flicking through the contents of a pornographic channel on the dedicated FO computer.

"Nothing, nothing that would interest you" Philip said

emphatically. "Just some information I was after."
"If you mean the price of coke," said the *attache*, easing his underwear, "I know a place...good lord, look at those!" And he lost his train of thought when confronted with such amplitude.

However, Philip took to the back streets. He had overcome the altitude sickness that strikes many visitors, not just fat Europeans, when they first arrive in Bogota and felt that he was a virtual native. True, his understanding of the language was poor, he being of the old Foreign Office school of foreign languages- speak English, loud and slow, as if for a deaf imbecile but most of the locals spoke American and looked upon him as a holy fool.

He had tried much of the wonderful night life when he first came and knew what he liked, namely the *Andres Carne de Res* restaurant, but he did not feel that this glamorous spot would provide him with the information that he sought. So it was to the other end of the city that he was making his way, pushing through the after-dinner crowds on a Thursday night, when he felt himself blocked by two backs in front of him.

"Brake, indicate, attempt three point turn-"

But before he could move, he felt two very hard pointy things in his back.

'Guns' weren't the first thing to come to his mind.

Ever since the terrible death of Georgi Markov, those in Philip's profession- and despite all his automotive inclinations, he was a professional diplomat down under- had feared the prospect of a rolled umbrella. However, having thought briefly and realising that whoever it was with whatever they had prodding in his back was too close for an umbrella, and anyway, it was a balmy night, Philip's next thought was ' not sharp enough for knife, so 'guns'"

But he was a British diplomat.

"I say," he said very loudly and in English," Do you mind!"

A voice in his ear said:" You shut uppa your face, eh? We not gonna hurt you." This was a relief until the voice in the other ear, accompanied by a devastating breath which displayed the owner's predilection for garlic sausage and beer, said:"Yet."

"Follow my brothers."

"I'm afraid I haven't had the pleasure of making the

acquaintances of..."

"The two boys in front."

Philip did as he was told with the two brothers in front pushing their way through the exuberant crowd, celebrating the fact that it was Thursday night and would soon be Friday night, another cause for revelry, turned into a side alley. Philip wasn't sure if he was to follow them until two prods from behind encouraged him.

"Terribly sorry- they didn't indicate."

It could have been out of a film, unshaven foreigners kidnapping a sweaty British agent in the middle of a riotous evening's entertainment, abroad in somewhere sweaty. The only thing was that Philip wasn't an agent and had no information of interest to foreign powers or international criminals. 'They would discover this soon enough and let me go' was what was going round his brain as the escort halted at the archetypal door with the obligatory grill which when opened, only displayed a blood-shot eye. This was unlocked from within and Philip nudged to enter.

The interior was not what he had expected; he had expected grim poverty, bare boards, adobe walls and a single lamp bulb hanging from a wire with massive bluebottles circulating. Instead, it could have been one of the better sets of rooms at an Oxbridge college, panelled in what could well have been mahogany -after all, on this side of the ocean it was more accessible than oak- with book-filled cases lining the walls, a couple of leathern arm chairs, a fine desk with, on one either side, two chairs which could well have graced the High table at the same college. Seated on one was a handsome middle-aged Colombian whom Philip thought to have seen before. He wore a perfectly cut tweed jacket, despite the evening heat.

"Ah, Mister de Courtney. You must excuse the manner in which my boys collected you but it is *de rigeur* in this part of town. Had you come by limo, everyone would have noticed but under duress, nobody raises an eyelash."

"Brow."

"What?"

"The expression is usually 'raised an eyebrow' but yours is..ah...finer. More refined."

"I'm getting rusty. It's a long time since I was up."

"Pardon?"

" At Oxford."

Philip was genuinely impressed. "I was at the other place- Fenners Polytechnic. Philip de Courtney- no, but of course, you must know my name. " And he held out a hand.

The other did not rise to the bait. Instead, he asked:

" But what I do not know is why you should want to be so keen to get involved with our terrible crop. But, just before you explain, I must say, I have an old friend who has the same name than you."

"As-" Philip was about to correct the man but decided not to muddy the waters yet, so continued:"-stounding. Called Philip? Well, it's not-"

"No," corrected the grandee," No Philip. 'de Courtney'. And what is even more amazing is, I had a postcard from him, jus' the other day from a place in Corn Wall." Foreigners never could get the intonation right.

"He say :" He searched in the top drawer and found the card- with a so-called Cornish milkmaid who appeared to have forgotten her vest on the front.

"My old friend, he and me, we have similar interests, see?

"Si," replied Philip.

"No I mean, see, look,." And he pressed a bell and a magnificent local girl with a similar abhorrence of underwear to the milkmaid appeared from a door in the bookcases.

"What you like-? " which reduced Philip to a fit of coughing until she finished-"To drink?"

"Do you think I could have a cup of tea?"

"No, please," said the grandee. "Our tea, it is virgin's water. Do try something local. Matia, two Cocos Loco."

She flashed a smile which the rest of her echoed more languorously.

"So, first you must know, I am Don Alfonso Cortes. I am not official official, but I am, shall we say?, 'near' to the government, so some things I can do, but not all. Next, I need to know- is it your family, the one of my dear friend, Cosmo?"

"Cosmo? You know uncle Cosmo? Remarkable- he rarely leaves Mena Dhu now-"

"But this was back thirty years . Only just after Falklands, so all us South Americas were 'argies'!" and he pronounced the word with all the venom of a BNP member from

Millwall.

"We South Americans had to be careful. I study at Oxford, some research , you understand-but that mean nothing to your... patriots who never been nearer to las Malvinas than Brighton!! Still, enough of that. Your Uncle Cosmo- he is a true Englishman and we two. we share the appreciation of the highest form of art- the female figure." Here Maria returned with the two drinks and Antonio tapped her appreciatively ,if incorrectly, on her bottom as she left.

"There was a club..."and here he repeated the story that young Sir Cosmo had told Lady Olivia but a few weeks previously. Finally:

"When his money run out and my people recall me, we say we meet again. That was nearly thirty years ago. And now, out of the blue sky, I get a postcard saying-." And here he turned it over.

" 'Cousin Philip in Embassy- please make welcome.' Then my people say me that you are Cousin Philip and you asking questions that don't usually get asked by your..how you say...'ancestors'? No-'forebears'? Not done before? Why?"

And so Philip explained his cryptic request. "They want to know how much it would cost to buy ten kilos of the.. um..'stuff' over here so that's the info I'm after."

, Aboard *HMS Runcorn*, the tannoy blurted: CPO Thomas, report to captain's cabin, CPO Thomas, report to captain's cabin.

Jim Thomas , Jenny's son, was an engineer aboard *the Runcorn*, a job that he loved. Being an Offshore Patrol Vessel, her crew worked a rota of two months on, one month off when in local waters but one of the many things that Jim liked about the job was trips like the one they were on at the moment, visits to the Caribbean and the previous year, to the Med. True, the job out there hadn't been very nice; they had had to help to try to deal with the endless flow of illegal immigrants and each one they came across was a tragedy in miniature but as he wrote to his mother: "Where else would would get paid to go island hopping in Greece or cruising the Caribbean?."

"Ah, Chief, " said Lieutenant Commander Macintosh, the officer commanding HMS Runcorn, as Jim entered his day cabin. "Have you been this way before?"

"Not Colombia, sir. More up Nicaragua way."

"Any idea why we're going? I know my opposite number on HMS Mersey was dying to go and was totally pissed off when their Lordships changed their minds and sent us instead."

"Maybe they realise at last that we deserve a bit of a knees up. I believe Carthagena is a bit more lively than Portsmouth."

"Impossible not to be, no, but I just get the feeling that this comes from pretty high up- all the way, even. You can't imagine why, can you? D'you think old Hawkins could be involved- the old bloke lives in your village now, doesn't he?"

"Well, yes but I can't imagine... I mean, he's a bit old for my mum. I think she's fifty but won't admit to it- if she goes on knocking years off, my birth will have been a minor miracle. But ninety-two or whatever- he's not going to want to have his end away at ninety two, is he?"

"I sincerely hope that if I get that far, I'll still have most bits working, although I do think I'd prefer to lose me powers of reproduction than me powers of thought, or speech. "said the Captain.

The next time Don Alfonso made contact with Philip de Coverlet was when he sent a very large American limousine to pick him up from the Embassy. Philip delighted in the workings of the choice of his transport but rather doubted the advisability. It was rather obvious.
"Isn't it rather obvious?" he said, when he saw don Alfonso.
"Not in Bogota. "
"It is for the British. Best we can do is a clapped-out Daimler."
"So," said don Alfonso; "Let us not beat up the bush- I feel sure we could find you some product. And, even though you are not the business *attache* , you will want to know the price. No?"
"Well, that is rather..."
" These day, it is always price, price, price. Very sad, no? You remember the summer of love? No? Nor me. It is all your Lady Thatcher's market forces. Pah!"
"There is one thing. It might be a problem- might affect the

price." And he handed the other a recent overseas copy of 'The Times,' open at the obituary page.

Don Alfonso started to read and gradually, tears filled in his eyes.

"I say," said Philip. "Are you all right? "

"Si," said Alfonso, sniffling, "Is just, my mother, she die last year. And this Lady..?"

"She's a cousin, and the whole thing about the hall was her idea- they needed the...product, to sell, To build a new one."

At this, don Alfonso gave up and collapsed into floods. "Is so ..beautiful. The product? You got it. No charge!"

"No charge!" exclaimed young Sir Cosmo, spluttering on his Sugar Puffs.

"No charge," said Hives over the phone.

"No charge?" echoed the Admiral, as he took his morning coffee.

"Michael?" repeated Mrs Guthrie." No, I'm afraid Michael is in London. Rehearsing. At Abbey Road, you know. Isn't that exciting?!"

"Not half as exciting as the news we've just had. Can you contact him there?"

"No charge? In Bolivia? But that's...amazing!" cried Michael. And he waltzed Sandy round Abbey Road's Studio 3. She had come to listen and was loving what she was hearing. With this news, she couldn't think of a time when she had been happier.

Andy and the Cross brothers had been very welcoming, all three secretly delighted to see that, finally, Michael was coming out of himself and obviously, this not-too-young lady was all part of the process. As were the new songs.

Chapter 19

They had run through the back catalogue quite easily; it was like riding a bike: once you had played your chart-toppers three hundred times, all over the world, there was little falling-off. It was when they came to the latest songs that Michael had written that things became so time-consuming. They were lovely but the melodies complex, demanding a complex backing and all four friends were determined to get these right.

When they reported the generous gesture from don Alfonso's people back in Bolivia to the committee, it was suggested that they might put up some sort of plaque but after a brief discussion, decided that it was probably not a very good idea.

The work on the new hall was going on apace and the Mechanicals could even rehearse their lines in tea breaks, when the Vicar came to call. Amongst the wood shavings and concrete mixers, people would hear:" Nay, faith, let me not play a woman; I have a beard coming " while H would provide an unsuitable ribald critique.

They were sitting out in front of the would-be hall on stacks of breeze blocks. If there was one thing 'H' was expert at, it was laying breeze blocks. Bricks needed a little more refinement but when you had forearms strong enough to rip a rugby ball from out of a Redruth maul- the laws were different in those days- then it was no surprise. 'H' was half way through a king-sized pasty his wife had made fresh that morning.

"An' if there's one thing my missus is good at- and I'll tell'ee, there's fuckin' more n'one, but if there's one thing, 'tis pasties. Nice bit o' shin, taties, onion and turnip. I knows they calls it ' swede' up country but we in't eatin' fuckin' Scandiwegians- tis 'turnip'. And none o' yer fuckin' carrot!" And he was about to return the pastie to his mouth having used it to emphasize his point when there was a crash of feathers, a hellish squawk and a black-backed seagull came in out of the sun over his right shoulder, slashed a scratch under 'H's eye with his lethal beak and flew off with the food in its beak.

"Bastard!" 'H' called after him. "Fuckin'..." He was lost for any other words. "That fuckin' fucker could'a fuckin' 'ad my fuckin' eye out!" He excelled himself. He dabbed at the cut with a filthy hankie.

"Let me have a look," Trevor who was there ready for a line rehearsal after lunch had a first-aider's certificate and the site always had a green case somewhere.

He dressed what was no more than a scratch.

"Any deeper, it could have been nasty."

"Nasty? I'll fuckin' give 'en 'nasty'. No-"He stood up once the vicar had finished. "Anyone see which way the bugger went?"

Jago had watched carefully-he had an idea what 'H' would do next.

"That one up on the ridge of the roof. The one as is laughin'"

"Right."

'H' opened his work-bag and took out a special Tuppaware box with a skull and cross bones on the lid. From within that, he took out what appeared to be a couple of normal sandwiches, made with white bread. He tore these in half and squeezed them together into smallish balls. He then pretended to eat one, watching his attacker all the while. The bird watched him, took off and prepared to swoop when 'H' seemed to make it all the easier for him by lobbing the bread into the air in front of the bird. He couldn't fail to catch it.

"Give 'im a couple and chuck out the others for luck," he said.

" Bless my soul," said Trevor. "That seems to be remarkably Christian of you. Almost turn the other cheek."

"You know me, Trev. 'Eart of gold."

"Things is, Vicar", said Jago. "What you don't know is they'm bicarb butties. Bicarbonate of Soda? And you know what that's for?"

Trevor was no cook.

"Makes the dough to rise. That rises inside that fucker, got nowhere to go and boom! Blows 'en to Kingdom Come! Though I doubt the Almighty will welcome 'im. Just 'ope the bits lands in the harbour. Otherwise 'e might just mess up our nice new brickwork.!"

Jenny was having a hard time with the Bard.

Rosemary Guthrie was making an excellent Lady Capulet but Mavis was struggling, unsurprisingly.

" 'I'll look to like if looking liking move'. I mean, like, what does it mean?"

"Well," said Jenny, who was no scholar,"um...? Rosemary?"

"Sort of- ok, I'll have a look if you think that by looking at him, I might like him."

"That's ace, Miss. Can you come and teach us?"

"No, dear- I've got one child to look after- well, two really. They're enough to be going on with"

Michael did not want to join the hard core of the committee- to which the Vicar and Jeremy had become attached- after the meetings in the pub and so invited Sandy back to the Garden House for cocoa.

"As long as it's not a euphemism," she had said.

"No, no" and then he paused. "But I'm told it might be an aphrodisiac!"

"Better not, then"

But Michael had prevailed and they were sitting with a

considerable breakfast bar between them to discourage intimacy.

"So. Where did you learn to dive?"

"On holiday. In Greece. The best sensation, isn't it? With a old boy-friend- or that should be 'a former' -nothing 'old' about him- about ten years ago- but it all ended when we were out in Kephalonia and he found he preferred his snorkel to me. He stayed and opened a dive-school off a beach just north of Sami and takes processions of sun-baked tourists to sit on the bottom of the sea for half an hour at a time. They think they're Jacques Cousteau and he screws the German or English girls whose partners have had too much sun. Or retzina. Or both."

"Have you always been a teacher?"

"I'm one of those terrible parasites who loved the three years at uni- Exeter- sorry, hate that word 'uni', specially as an English student-."

She corrected herself.

"'University', had no idea what to do and so did a PGCE - primary school-to put off the dreaded decision for another year and luckily got sent to some tiny place like this one but on the north coast for teaching practice, and actually liked teaching little ones. The best thing in the world."

"So that's two best things already- diving and teaching little ones- ."

"Sorry," said Sandy, "I'm just not used to talking about myself. Must be the cocoa."

She blushed as he put out a hand.

" You're the first girl I've really talked with since...Joanna."

"Do you want to talk about her?"

They looked at each other, And then a voice came from a figure framed in the door.

"Hey, are you going to kiss her or me first? I'm trying not to fall asleep!"

It was Jake, wearing a small T shirt from the Angels' last tour and a pair of Spiderman boxer shorts silhouetted against the corridor light.

"Oh, Jake, "cried Michael,"I am SO sorry! I promised I'd come up and kiss him good night when I got back from the meeting."

"It's my fault, Jake,"said Sandy. "Your dad was being very hospitable-"

"Michael doesn't know nothing about hospitals," said Jake, grumpily.

"It doesn't mean that-it means..er..'welcoming'."

"But can't he be welcoming when he's been and tucked me in."

Michael picked up his son and carried him upstairs. All the while, the boy clung to his father and looked rather apprehensively at their guest.

But when he had been put in his mezzanine bunk with the work station built in below and the pirate panda duvet pulled up over him and his father hugged and kissed him, he asked: "Can Miss Sandy kiss me 'good night' too?"

Sandy checked Michael's face; he nodded so she placed a gentle kiss on the child's forehead.

"Good night, Jake. "

Then Michael took her back downstairs but this time to the living room; the fire had died down, so he put another couple of logs on, patted the sofa beside him and started :

" I met Joanna in San Francisco. At the Ritz-Carlton Millennium thrash." "

When Rosemary Guthrie came down from her flat in the

attic to say 'good night', she took one look in through the door and didn't bother.

Trevor was most surprised to find Letitia Butt on her mobility scooter out at Olivia's grave in the churchyard at St Wallow's.

"Mrs. Butt. I-we didn't even know you were down. Jeremy would have..."

"No, Vicar,"she said but there was only a trace of the old imperious blustering. "No, I managed. And perhaps a graveyard is a suitable place to describe. what I can only call..a damascene moment.!"

Trevor wasn't quite sure what she meant.

"Saul on the road to Damascus.? Remember? Or more mundane but far more apt, perhaps, Scrooge after those four Christmas spirits."

Again, Trevor wondered if it was spirits of a more prosaic type until she said: "It's all about the money. The parable of the talents. I was the one who thought I was being a good servant by squirrelling away what I'd got. But really, in some...perverted way, I was enjoying going without. But ever since whoever it was paid my debts, I've started spending money. Having to. And I love it! I used to try to persuade myself that I was saving it for the children, as some sort of custodian- but that's tommyrot. They never came to see me so I decided they can bally well look after themselves, and so I'm spending their inheritance and loving it. Buying good wine, Berry Brothers and Rudd rather than those awful boxes from the supermarket and getting out to street markets on the scooter rather than counting on Harrods to send in something decent in their hampers. And the thing is, ever since the grub's been better, the sprogs have been inviting themselves and all their families round to dinner! Something in Ecclesiastes about that, isn't there? " Cast thy bread upon the waters: for thou shalt find it after many days." Well, it wasn't so much bread as a rather rare Beef Wellington and a few bottles of Regnier Beaujolais and it didn't take that many days either!"

The old lady was transformed. Gone were the Giles' granny hat, those affected cloaks and heavy tweeds. Instead she was actually wearing trousers, a Burberry cashmere jumper and a very theatrical pashmina in shot silver. Her hair was a natural white and she wore a little make-up, finely powdered.

"How are you getting on with your scooter?"

"Loving it, dear boy, loving it. I'm no longer lonely- I'm independent"

"I shall have to tell the Admiral; he's always on the look-out for additions to his formation team, especially since Mrs. Allen has been done for speeding."

She smiled, although wasn't really sure what he was talking about. After a pause:

" Oh!"said the Vicar. "I'm sorry if I interrupted your...." He gestured towards Lady Olivia's grave, the earth still dark and moist and only the headstone to show who lay below.

"No, no- I've come down to write. If I'm to read at your festival, I've decided I can't do any of the old stuff. So I've come out to commune with Olivia in search of inspiration."

"Any luck?"

"Well", said the old lady with a rare smile," the old grey matter is churning- we shall see if anything comes out pat!"

No soon had she made it under her own steam back to the cottage when there was a perfunctory knock and Cyril Oliphant insinuated himself round the door.

"Oh, Letitia, I heard you were back- does little Mou-mou need walkies? "

He looked about expectantly.

"No, as there is no longer a little Mou-mou for you to drag round the village until the poor thing peed. I realised that the only reason I was keeping her was because there was no-one else who would listen to me. I had her put out of her suffering."

"Surely living with you was not suffering?"

"Just about everybody else thought it was."

Cyril pulled up a stool, picked up the notes and dictionaries that Letitia was using, deposited them on the floor and sat himself on the stool.

"Look, what are we going to do about this festival of theirs?"

Mrs Butt looked at him. And the comparison with the conversion of St Paul continued as she recalled: 'And immediately there fells from his eyes as it had been scales.' For the first time, she realised what an awful person he was, that his leather jacket could easily have been confused for a plastic reproduction while the collarless shirt looked really old and tatty rather than stylishly distressed. The cords were still maroon, sparking the suggestion that they may be the only pair that he possessed. The rimless glasses exaggerated the veins in the eyeballs and he really did look like a startled hare (without the ears.).

"I know what I'm going to do," she replied calmly. "I've been invited to read some of my work. What about you? First thing you're going to do is pick up all my stuff, Thank you. Put it back where you found it, where I was working on it. I mean, what work do you actually do?. And none of that cod's wallop about GCHQ. I am in touch with a number of retired Civil Servants with fingers in all those sorts of pies and they have never heard of you. "

"I-, I-ah, I...if that's how you're going to repay all..." He was floundering

"Which reminds me- did you ever use my name to gain credit in the shop?"

Cyril shut the door quickly behind him.

Letitia returned to her notes, and muttered:

' Oh broken village,
Wounded in thy flank
Thy main street pillaged
And assailed point-blank.
Mother Nature.....' What can we say about Mother Nature in iambic pentameters?"

Jenny insisted that they did that scene from 'the Tempest ' when Miranda first sees the passengers from the wrecked ship and says 'O brave new world that hath such people in't!' with Jeremy as Prospero, Mavis as Miranda, Bobby as Ferdinand, and the Vicar as Alonso.

When Tegan heard, down on the beach with Bobby that he was going to have to go topless, she said that it was just so Jenny could have her 'Poldark' moment,

" Remember the harvesting with the shirt off?Jennie says that the buffeting of the waves in the wreck would have torn it off," said Bobby who didn't have to say much in the scene, just look handsome.

"Carrying that to its logical conclusion," said Tegan, "Why didn't the sea rip off his breeches as well! That would have opened Miranda's eyes!"

"I don't think Porthwallow is ready for full frontal nudity." said Bobby.

"Won't miss much," said Tegan, who then had to dive onto the sand to avoid the on-rushing laughing young man.

Chapter 20

Jim had finally received a letter from his mother, which, in itself was strange, as she seemed to much prefer Skype these days, once the village was finally connected to broadband... She had hinted at things over the last few conversations but now there it was in black and white.

"When you get to C. someone will contact you. Admiral Bobby's plan. Please tell no-one unless you have to. Details as to delivery to follow, somehow. Hope you can be home for end of August. Big event in the village. love, your mum."

The arrival of HMS Runcorn into the naval base at Bocagrande, Carthagena, was cause, if cause were needed, for celebration. The only thing was, you had to take it easy and pace your celebrations; it is at sea level- of course, it's a naval base- but quite a shock after Bogota, at 2650 meters higher up on the plateau and 20 degrees when Cartagena has an average temperature of 28 degrees, centigrade. So, instead of altitude sickness, hangovers.

Philip seemed to be melting, permanently. Rather like some never-ending antic Greek punishment when the eagles would peck ceaselessly at parts of one's anatomy or a rock have to be rolled eternally up hill, so Philip sweated."Top up radiator, battery fluid, windscreen wash daily, if not more so. Park in the shade."

He had no idea how they did it but don Alfonso's fraternal snatch squad from Bogota materialized around him as soon as he stuck his panama-hatted head outside the front door of the British Consulate on Carrera 13b- the city was designed as a grid and so, in theory, it is difficult to get lost here.

"I say, chaps-" but they all but carried him to a car parked as near as possible. Sadly, everywhere in the world these days, parked cars are looked upon with great suspicion and liable to be blown up, either by the authorities or by those who parked them there.

This time it was within the Old City that they went and even in car mode and anxious as to what might happen next, Philip could not fail to be amazed by the old walls, the restaurants and bars and even more so, the 16th century cathedral.

. They slowed down to a lazy walk because one of the open

horse-drawn carriages had pulled out in front . These seemed to be a popular mode of transport with lovers, or at least members of the opposite sex out together as they took in all the sights. The bodyguards quickly expelled Philip from the car and deposited him into the back of the carriage in front where, no longer surprised by anything, he found don Alfonso and a comely senorita. What was remarkable was that don Alfonso was also accompanied by two llamas. Or they might be alpacas, Philip was no expert.

"These are for you, don Philipe, " said don Alfonso who watched the horrified look on Philip's face with amusement. " No- don't worry- not yet- and they are toys. You know what your British police call those who carry 'coca' on their person? 'Mules'. Sorry, we don't have mules - we have llamas instead!"

Philip's horror increased until he realised that it was a Colombian joke.

"We are gonna give your splendid Navy fellows free alpaca-toys for their little ones at home-*para las nina* regular, toy alpacas, free. They jus' have to carry them on board . No bother. An' your man, he will have two alpacas;

coupla kilo of product in each. You think he can find somewhere safe to put them in his boat?"

Philip was bemused, not only by the heat, but also by the prospect of smuggling cocaine on to an actual Royal Naval drug-buster.

'Coals to Newcastle' briefly passed through his mind and then he realised that even that was not enough. 'Daniel in the bloody lions' den' came next.

"Well, I don't really know, I haven't met him yet."

That happened the next evening during the reception on board the Runcorn. Whenever the British Fleet visit a port in the Caribbean, they hosted a drinks party for local bigwigs or whichever British politicians had wangled a freebee in that part of the world. Fortunately it was only a few from the Embassy who joined the Colombian politicians; they all knew each other from other piss-ups in Bogota and it was something of a short straw to be send to one of these thrashes in Cartagena. They mostly drank lemonade, knowing the effects of too much booze in extreme heat.

Jim had a chance to check the guest list and when he

saw Philip de Courtney, felt there could be no doubt. The only problem was finding our which of the Brits was his fellow conspirator without going round and propositioning them all. That way disaster could lie.

However, as they come up the gangway off the dock, there could really only be one contender : while all the others were as immaculate as the heat allowed in white tuxedos and snowy shirts, Philip was still in his usual crumpled suit and clutching the battered panama . Almost as soon as his feet had touched the deck and he had shaken Lieutenant-Commander Macintosh's hand, he downed in one the first glass offered by the steward and reached for another.

Jim eased his way through the growing crowd on the after deck.

"Excuse me"

" Slam on the anchors. Handbrake. What?!" This man was obviously anxious about something.

"I'm from Porthwallow. "

"Lucky chap- wish I was there- oh, you.re...?" And he winked very conspicuously.

"Chief Petty Officer Thomas, sir. I hear they're having a bit of a shindig back 'ome." His Cornish origins could still be heard

"Sssh, ssh." Philip took another enormous swallow from his glass which emptied it. Jim beckoned to another steward.

"God, they've got some balls back home. Either that or no-one's worked out that it is somewhat ironical that we should be trying to transport five kilos of the old snow on board a drug-buster!"

Jim nearly choked ,

"What!?"

"Yes. " Then he switched t a cod American accent . "And your mission, Jim should you choose to accept it , is to get the stuff back to British waters. You don't have to worry about landing it- just get it somewhere near home. I shall self-destruct in five seconds."

"Can we talk abut this?"

"Do you have any shore leave?"

"Tomorrow afternoon, but..."

"Can you be at the dock gates at two? "

"I expect so.

"And don't be surprised by who comes to fetch you. Or what in!" Whereupon he refused the guided tour, saying that he'd been round the one last year and didn't expect they'd have changed much.

Jim was dressed in what civvies he had that were suitable for such heat and humidity but the British had a long history of overdressing. He was pouring sweat just standing at the dock gates but fortunately, the air-conditioned limo was on time.

"Senor Thomas,"asked the driver.

"Yes?"

"Please to get in."

"You must understand," said don Alfonso when he met with Philip and Jim at the back of an Old Town cafe, so far back that the heat was considerably diminished.." that this is not our normal line of work. Quantity, price, all very different and of course, we cannot use our usual ..ah..modes of transport. Here your '*almirante*' and of course, the family of the late Lady have all offer so much help. Our little *presente* is nothing special-"

"Ah, but it is, " said Philip. "Have you heard," this to Jim, "Have you heard that they're giving it to us? As a present. In memory of Aunt Olivia.!? If only she could write and thank-" and then he realised the pointlessness of what he was saying. "Ah. No."

Jim was speechless. Alfonso continued:

"And I enjoy not only the giving but, same as with what I enjoy most about my job every day- logistics. This is the right word, no? Getting one thing from one place to another safely and on time.?"

"Yes, sir," said Jim, "We have officers in the British Navy who do nothing but. Not organise drug smuggling, of course, but logistics, yes- that's what they call themselves. Every ship will have one. I bet ours would love to offer his help but..."

"No, I don't think so."

"No, come to think about it, maybe not. But I can appreciate the challenge."

"In that case, can you get five or six of your sailors, ideally older, with children to come ashore tomorrow evening.

With you?"

When Jim returned to *the Runcorn* that night, accompanied by five hand-picked mates, mostly from the engine room and each over thirty with at least one real child, there was a mix of laughter on board, from sniggers to open guffaws. Each of the six was carrying a raffia alpaca with a straw sombrero on its head.

When they had met the kind man who explained that he was from the Government which was trying to improve the image of their country with the world in general and that these toys were a gesture of that friendship, they accepted with gratitude. Don Alfonso took Jim aside and gave him a smaller package. "These are a local delicacy. Leave them in your cabin."

Jim had learned to question nothing .

As each of the six sailors passed the guard on the gate, they repeated the phrase that they had been taught :"Para los ninos"-('for the children'). The first was regarded with suspicion but the amusement grew as the next and the next passed, so that by the time that Jim arrived with his two not-obviously heavy toys, he was waved through. For a second, he thought he had succeeded but :

"Momentito."

He stopped and it took all his determination to keep the silly grin on his face.

"Dos?" asked the guard, "Two?"

The inspiration struck.

"I have twins."

The other laughed and explained to his *amigo* :" Mellizos. Mellizos. Twin!" and waved him through.

The hall was progressing so well that Jenny Thomas was even more snowed under than usual.. As she saw it, not only was she producing the whole event- ok, there were all the other committee members but she was shouldering the responsibility (unbeknownst to the others) Then there was directing the Shakespeare entertainment. At times, she referred to them as 'gobbets' or 'bleeding chunks' and, ignoring the fact that those in each scene seemed to have everything completely under control, agonized about them. And now, as the only person in the village with any real experience of the technical side of theatres, she was worrying about equipping their new stage.

She accepted that Michael had played in just about every theatre all over the world from the Round House back in the 90s in London to the Maple Leaf Gardens in Toronto and the Madison Square Garden in New York since the Millennium but felt sure that he hadn't have to hang the lights and draw the curtains himself.

"Tell you who you should talk to, " suggested Bobby, interrupting Jenny's laments during one their sub-committee meetings in the pub.

"Who?"

"The Man who lives in the Woods."

"What? The old Paynter chap?"

"I'd heard he worked at the Aldwych- In London. That's a proper theatre, isn't it? They must have had people to hang lights and draw curtains. " He glanced over at Tegan who was the spit and image of innocent ignorance.

"And Stratford."

"Well....if someone can contact him...somehow. We'll postpone the subject of lighting and sound until the next meeting. Or we can always call an extraordinary meeting..."

"What'd be 'extraordinary' about it? " asked Henry, who only ever saw Jack when he came in for a bottle of cider and some bread.

"Jack coming into the village."

But Jack disappointed them when Tegan and Bobby went to invite him into a meeting.

"I'm no great shakes at committee meetin's, specially consid'rin' some a the people you'd be meetin' with. But if you got a pencil an' paper, I'll give 'ee a name.'Ansum. 'E used to work fer Arena Systems. Up Lunnun."

" Bran O'Farrell no longer works here ."

Bobby could imagine the sweep of blonde hair, starting above the left eye and going all the way around the head until it swooped to rest on her right shoulder, attempted by thousands, mastered by so few, that housed the honeyed. moneyed tones of the receptionist who delivered this disappointing piece of information.

"Well, thanks, anyway-.Bye."

"No- just a minute, " Cressida or Romilly or whatever her name was stopped him ringing off.

"Since his accident, he can't rig but he does still come in now and then. For the craic". The Irish origins stirred from beneath the layers of Knightsbridge pollen and waved lazily.

"Who shall I say called?"

"Well," said Bobby, "My name's Bobby Hawkins, but I'm calling on behalf of Jack Payne, an old friend of his."

Bran rang back within the hour,

"Bran O'Farrell. They said it was about auld Jack. The bugger isn't dead, I hope- he still owes me a fiver!" and the explosion of laughter belied any possible malevolence there might seem in the message.

Bobby explained .

"He was dead right. You've come to the right man. If you can fetch me from the station, I'll be on the next train to whichever god-foresaken hole it is you live in."

"But Mr O'Farrell, "-

"If you don't call me 'Bran', I shan't play!"

"Bran, we can't afford expert fees-"

"Then you've nothing to worry about, as I shan't charge them. Just find me a bed for the night and a crust of bread and a few hours to catch up with auld Jack, I'm happy. Are we on?"

The figure that Jeremy brought back this time from the station differed in almost every respect from the one he had fetched in February. Their one similarity was the crutch. Where his left leg should have been was a void.

"Don't worry, Jerry, I'll tell yous all about it. In the car. Is it a long way away, this Porthwallow?"

"About twenty years."

Bran O'Farrell loved the theatre, backstage rather than on it. He had started young in Galway but like anyone with aspiration , had headed for London. He got to know Jack in the last days at the Aldwych but whereas Jack went to Stratford, Bran joined a small lighting hire and rigging company..They had been in the van of the development of both moving lights and abseiling riggers, where the crew members would fly up and down rather than having to haul in and out a whole bar of lights (or lanterns), just to change a bulb (or lamp), in the profession's confusing jargon.

With the development of ever more refined computerised stage lighting and spectacular rock concerts, Arena Systems with Bran O'Farrell their star rigger went from strength to strength until they were the first name on any producer in Europe's list. Until the terrible day when like Icarus, Bran fell.

The insurance made him a rich man but he still craved the adrenalin-rush of an all-night fit-up and an opening night and so he stayed and helped where experience was more valuable than basic agility.

"And so," he said, as Jeremy pulled up, "Here I am," And then, after he had got out of the car and looked around at the glorious little village and its fishing quay, "Or have I died and gone to Heaven,?" and added,as Jenny bustled up, generating her usual aura of overworked efficiency "Sure and isn't this one of the angels."

It was instant. Despite his age, nearer sixty than fifty, and the piratical absence of a lower limb, the man generated animal attraction . The abseil rigging had produced a torso and shoulders of a gymnast while the mane of black and white hair was tied back with a headband and that Irish sparkle- "Sure an' if they could bottle it, they'd make a million" rarely failed.

While totally unexpected, he was exactly what Jenny needed, and after an evening in the pub, at which Jack Paynter mysteriously appeared and then just as quietly disappeared, . there was absolutely no opposition when Jenny said:"You my dear man, are coming home with me!"

It was fortunate her husband was away , halfway across Europe, with an artic. full of velvet crabs for Spain.

The next day, they sat down and made out a shopping list of internally-wired lighting bars, computerised control boards and a dozen of the latest lanterns.

"And tell you what- I'll come back and check up on the job as long as my boys from Arena can do it. There are none better. And possibly light your little concert too; we'll have to ask Michael. "

The local electricians were delighted not have to to mess about with theatre wiring, so everybody was happy.

Jenny, miraculously relaxed, in receipt of a list from an

expert and a good rogering from the same, had an enormous smile on her face for days, until her husband got home when she immediately checked his diary for his next long-distance run.

Chapter 21

Jim did not sleep well on the return crossing of the Atlantic, mainly because he had to share his cabin all the way with two cocaine-bearing raffia alpacas, christened Miguel and Lolita. Lieutenant- Commander Macintosh was surprised to see them on his inspection rounds but when Jim had explained that it was all part of that operation that had sent them there in the first place, Commander Macintosh thought no further of it, or if he did, presumed that that was the sort of thing you could order once you had been an admiral.

As they neared the Western Approaches, Jim took a knife to the alpacas and relieved them of their burden and replaced it with old pillows intentionally soiled with oil. The purser took a dim view .:
"I hate to think what you've been doing with these, Chief but whatever it was, I'm sure it would have been better if you'd have washed your hands after." Jim accepted the reprimand because, come what may, he intended taking Miguel and Lolita off that ship with him. He had become

fond of them and knew exactly who might appreciate them. Lolita was intended for his mother while Miguel was intended for his intended, who wasn't as yet aware of his intentions.

Then he taped the packages to a deflated rubber ring , in fact an inner tube, that had been sent via the Diplomatic Bag to the Embassy. And waited.

The Isles of Scilly passed out of sight on the port side, Brest on the starboard. Now was the time.

They had an air compressor in the engine room and while it was not its main reason for being there, it did help with blowing up balloons for their on-board receptions. The laden ring took no time at all.

Even at night and at such a distance, Lady Olivia's White House was visible; Jim felt an unusual pang of home-sickness but, like the good servant that he was, he had a job to do and do well. He chucked the ring as far away from the ship and was about to heave a sigh of relief when a voice spoke.

"What was that, Chief?"

An officer off watch was taking a breath of air.

"What?"

"What you tossed in back there."

"I know we shouldn't..." He was thinking fast when inspiration struck. "but you know the White House- I think we all know it's nearly Plymouth when we see it- well, the old lady who used to live there, she died a while back and this is the first time I've been past since. It's the village where I was born. It was...sort of, just like some flowers. . and stuff... my...well, my act of remembrance, sir. "

"Oh, I say...jolly good show. Carry on, chief."

As the stern of HMS Runcorn disappeared into the late evening twilight, heading for Portsmouth. there was even a little phosphorescence in her wake.

Then the black rib that had shot out from the bay in which it had been waiting drew nearer. They couldn't come too near or too fast or else they might have been taken for an in-coming torpedo. On board, steering, was Jago, an unfamiliar life-jacket around his neck He, like many of the fishermen was not a strong swimmer, the old adage being that an ability to swim simply made it longer to drown should you sink. Sandy and Michael were difficult to discern in wet suits.

As they neared the path of the warship, Jago flicked a switch on a little gizmo that he was holding, courtesy too of the admiral..

"There is is, "said Sandy as a little flashing light could be seen about a hundred yards away, echoed by a bleep on the handset.

"Best get it quick," said Jago,"Otherwise folks'll be thinking they put up another light'ouse."

The light of the Eddystone could be seen, flashing white twice every ten seconds and as their eyes got used to the darkness and as they looked around the horizon, so clear that night, they could begin to see several, some mere pin pricks far away west, other nearer and more obvious.

Jago drew the rib expertly alongside the massive inner tube, which Sandy held on to as Michael tried to heave the lot into the boat.

"Heavier than you think. Got a knife?," he whispered .

Jago drew the razor-sharp sliver of metal that he wore in

his boot for gutting fish. He cut the tape on the first bundles which fell safely into the bottom of the boat; however, somehow the teamwork didn't work on the next and one slowly toppled overboard.

"I"ll get it," and Sandy turned a neat backward somersault into the sea.

"Oh, bugger," said Michael and dived in after, following her down.

Fortunately the bundle was awkward and made attempts to float so Sandy had caught it quite quickly but was not making any headway in bringing it back to the surface. Michael was needed for that and he heaved it over the round rubber . The two of them clung to the side panting but smiling.

"What a team!" said Jago, honestly impressed.

They ran the rib into Talland Bay where no matter what the tide, there was always a little sand. The winding Cornish lanes were a nightmare by day when visitors from upcountry would either drive as if they were still on the A 38, far too fast, or like terrified rabbits, unable to move unless in the middle of the lane; however, t here was the black Daimler parked on the fringe of the beach as the rib nosed the sand. Jago leaped over the side to hold the boat stern on the what waves there were, while Sandy handed the bags to Michael over the side. Like magic, two figures dressed as though they were delivering Milk Tray, appeared beside Michael.

"Bugger me, mate, these roads! Ain't even lanes- fuckin' dirt tracks, some of 'em. Give me Wandsworth any day."

"You'll be ok" replied Michael," you should be back in about five hours."

"Five? Only took us three and a half to get here. And an hour of that was from Plymouth."

"Well, don't get done for speeding. That's the last thing we need."

"Say no more."

The men in black carried the bags up the beach, put them in the boot of the car and drove off, very carefully.

While the three in the rib returned to Porthwallow.

There was a real feeling of satisfaction; they had nearly done it.

They were tying up and about to go their own ways. "What a team," Jago repeated. "Hey, do you want any of this?" And he held up a plastic bag.

"What you got there? Drugs?! Smile!"

It was Cyril Oliphant, taking a photo with his phone..

However what Jago was offering was fish.

"Hooked on fish?"

He had had a line of feathers over the side while they had been waiting for the *Runcorn* and picked up half a dozen mackerel and a very nice gurnard. If one can call a fish 'nice' that has a head like a stone sphynx and skin like sand-paper.

"You want some?" asked Jago, hauling the gurnard out of the plastic bag. Jago always gutted his catch as soon as it was in the boat so the fish was still bloody.

"Oh, I thought-"

"Well, here you are!"

He slapped Cyril across the chops with the gurnard several times and in a moment of genius, shoved it head first down the maroon cords. And wiggled it.

" Free of charge; that makes very good eating once you've

got its head off- just mind the pricks. Motto for all of us."

Cyril stumbled away into the night, clutching his groin. They waited a moment and then all three burst out laughing.

"Well," said Jago. "I'm away to me bed." And when he turned back and watched the other two, arm in arm, heading out to the Garden House, thought:"An' I' ope you are too."

Next morning, when Jake came into the '*en suite*' bathroom which separates his room from Michael's, he saw two wetsuits on the floor and decided that now was not a good time to go and wake his father.

When the *Runcorn* finally docked and the ship was routinely inspected for drugs, the Black German Shepherd, known as Star suddenly reacted passing Jim's cabin.

"What we got here then, Chief?" said the supercilious handler.

"Nothing special- I really don't think the dog..." But before Jim could speak, the dog had found the package given to Jim in Bolivia. Which sent Star yowling away, trying to run and wipe her nose with her paws at the same time

Jalepino peppers were one of Boliva's major legal exports and while ideal as a present for a foodie, they are not suited for the finely-tuned olfactory organ that is a sniffer dog's nose, completely obliterating the slightest trace of cocaine that might have remained.

"I'd like to call the sixth Porthwallow Village Hall Reconstruction Committee to order."

"Point of order, Mister Chairman." It was Jeremy, almost the first time that he had spoken in any of the meetings.

" I hate to interrupt unnecessarily but, as you so rightly say, this is the sixth meeting but, so far, you have given the committee six different names at the start. I may be an old fuddy-duddy-"

"Seconded!" came from the Vicar.

"Out of order; ignore that last remark, sorry, Jeremy, do go on."

" I'll have words with you later," he said to Trevor, only half in jest." You may feel it irrelevant but I should welcome the mood of the meeting as to whether we should standardize the name. For posterity. "

"What name do you wan to call it?"

"Whichever you prefer, as long as we have a majority choice. It's rather like Brexit- it doesn't matter how ludicrous as long as the majority gets it right."

Which was why the headings of each set of minutes was scored through and Porthwallow Village Hall Reconstruction Committee replaced them.

"Only one item on the agenda tonight- the running order for the Festival."

"Excuse me," interrupted Sandy." Michael sends his apologies. I'm not quite sure why but the band has had to go to Plymouth Docks."

"Well, we can work backwards," said Jenny, " I'm presuming- I imagine we all are, that Michael and the Angels are closing the show?"

" Somehow," said the Admiral, " Michael and I've been discussing it. Think it's all under control. I should take it as read. What I want to know is when POEMS is going to appear."

"If you mean Letita..." started the Vicar but the old man

interrupted .
"No, no- she'd a pretty moveable feast, as it were. I mean Poems, P.O.E.M.S- Porthwallow Over Eighties Mobility Squad!"

It was agreed that they should open the event. Then if as still might happen, Mr Collard was confused by the crowd, the bales of straw would still be in place to stop him veering into the harbour. However, when it came to deciding upon an order for the various Scenes from Shakespeare, real hostility arose. The rivalry between the Mechanicals and the Jennyt and Nurse scene cast was fierce and so they agreed simply to put 'Scenes from Shakespeare' into the poster and be no more specific than that. The various stalls, the coconut shy, the tombola and the soft toys, the maypole, Letitia's poetry reading-
"Mustn't clash with 'Sticking the Tail on the donkey' this time"remarked the Vicar, the perennial Punch and Judy man who false teeth made the understanding of the immutable dialogue more and more difficult each year, all these events filled the poster until it was noticed that there was no mention of Michael and the Angels.

"Shouldn't that be blazoned across the sky in letters of fire,?" asked Jenny, "Or at least written on the poster somewhere?!."

"I don't think he's worried about the poster," said Sandy whom everybody had tacitly accepted as Michael's spokes-person, " Just put,' Plus local band' or something like that at the bottom. His fans have twitter accounts, Facebook pages. As soon as it is announced anywhere, the whole world will know."

"And half of it want to come. Are we going to have to issue tickets?"

"I do think we should contact your friends the police, Jago. In case of traffic"

"Yeah, suppose. D'you want me to have word with Bert Drake? P'raps keep the emmets out. Reckon they'll be able to hear Michael down Looe or over Meva., if the Eden concerts is anything to go by" . Rock concerts held at the Eden Project, twenty miles away, could be heard of a summer's night- not very clearly but you could certainly sing along with the bass.

"And are the lavatories under control?"

"Yes,"replied Alf," 'Looby-loos'. Tis the name o the firm. Get it?"

"But what still worries me, is where are they goin' to play!?" said Henry, a practical man.

"Ah", said the Admiral who up until then had, like all good vice-presidents, sat at the back, kept quiet and ensured that others did the work, " I think I can safely say, having just had a signal from the officer commanding our Plymouth dockyard, that we do have a stage for them. As somebody once said, I believe, ' I just love it when a plan comes together'."

Chapter 22

The day dawned and the committee were up before dawn. The hay-bales to protect the public- and stop Mr. Collard from ending up in the harbour were in place. Much to Jenny's delight, Bran O'Farrell arrived in the passenger seat of an Arena Systems transit and oversaw the erection of a P.A. system to end all P.A. systems.

"Trouble is, darlin', yours was only one step up from two cocoa tins and a piece of string. When Ian here"- he pointed to the Adonis in the t-shirt commemorating the last Michael and the Angels tour who had been driving the van and who was unloading several flight cases on wheels," When Ian here, has finished, you'll not only be able to hear a fish fart but also determine what key it's in."

When they came to test it, Bran's "Good morning, Vietnam" could be heard up in the Admiral's house on the cliff , by the Man who Lives in the Woods in the woods and it disturbed the Vicar at his solitary morning prayer in church.

The committee's concern about visitor numbers were justified. The car park in the village was soon full so, in anticipation, Steve the farmer had harvested the two of his fields nearest to the village for overflow parking where he discovered his very enterprising teen-aged son charging £5 a car so that visitors would not have too far to walk.

"I presume that's going towards the 'all?" Steve asked.

"Yes, well- after costs." Everyone knows there is no such thing as a poor farmer.

As the visitors walked down to the quay, they had to pass the almost-finished hall and they all agreed that is was a very fine hall indeed.

Bert Drake drove out to the village with one of his fellow constables in the back. The passenger seat, as on that fateful morning back in February, was occupied by Inspector Foot in full uniform.

"D'you remember..?" Bert started but Foot interrupted.

"Absolutely. It's why I said I'll make up the numbers."

"You gonna 'elp with traffic up the 'ill, sir!?."

"I don't know about that, but I shall most definitely be part of the visible Constabulary presence. Probably on the quay."

Tegan at the pub was busy even before opening time as Bran had explained that any event like this runs on bacon sandwiches and coffee and once the crew had had their first, others discovered this delicacy and they had already had to send up to the shop for supplies. Henry was very busy behind the counter and had even persuaded Alma to come and help so Cheryl and Tina were sent down to deliver all that they had. Back to back, like secret agents defending each other in a foreign land, they edged their way through the crowd, never having seen so many people in the village before.

Even though they had not been ordered and the police would not let them into the village itself, several ice-cream vans had set up shop along the road.

The Lions' Club pig-roast had established itself at the far end of the quay and as the moment drew near, the members of the Porthwallow Community Fire Brigade informally but in uniform, because they liked their red shirts, spread among the front row of the crowd, to act as security.

"Remember Altamont?" Alf asked one of his younger colleagues, who had no idea what he was talking about.

The Vicar looked across the quay; he was dressed in his Peter Quince costume already but had kept his dog collar on, and very slightly, his left hand holding tight to Jeremy's beside him, sketched a cross and whispered a silent blessing.

Then a voice was heard: 'Here they come' and over the tannoy the Skaters' Waltz' could be heard as Mr. Collard led a cortege of seven mobility scooters, the pocket-battleship Admiral bringing up the rear.

Mr. Collard smiled and waved the the crowd, seeming to

be in a world of his own, which meant that his course bore no relation to the routine that they had so strenuously rehearsed but the old ladies- the rest, apart from the Admiral, were old ladies- worked on the elephant herd principle and simply followed the one in front. The crowd loved it.

The young followed the old, as was apt, and the youngsters from the school, under Sandy's tutelage, excelled themselves around the maypole.

Jeremy, the *eminence grise* behind the whole program, has brilliantly avoided the possibility of Letitia Butt's poetry reading clashing with the 'Pin the tail on the donkey' by asking her to run that stall as well, which she did with enormous gusto and a very blue running commentary.

At the end of that, revelling in the sound quality of Bran's PA system, she recited for the whole village to hear, her new poem.

Oh broken village,
Wounded in thy flank
Thy main street pillaged
And assailed point-blank.

Mother Nature groaned and suffered
Until thy people cried 'Enough-' Her
Hurts we'll dress, whate'er befall
And in its place, rebuild our Hall!

Those at the back thought that she had summed up the whole situation succinctly and started to clap but they did not know Mrs Butt."I haven't finished yet! " So she went on:

And so the doughty workers toiled
To mend what wind and rain had spoiled,
And now erected by their hands
Our brand-new Village Hall now stands
So let us now with heart and voice
Join as one and cry" Rejoice!
Porthwallow has a Village Hall
A place of fun for one and all."

The audience were uncertain this time so she added:

"I have finished this time.! "

This, as much as the verses themselves, were greeted with loud applause. However, the quality of the sound system could not fail to pick up 'H': "Le'ss jus' 'ope round the back o' the 'all's as much fun as the old un used ter be! Oh, bugger, we'm on next."

The Mechanicals would not have failed to bring the house down, had there been a house. And truth be told, all the Scenes from Shakespeare went well, only proving that the old boy knew a thing or two about the stage. Even Cheryl and Tina Lake, released from the shop by their parents, admitted that they were having a nice time, although this was immediately after Bobby's half-naked appearance as Ferdinand.

Cheyanne had brought her 'posse' of drama students, considerably enlarged in number from when Jenny had first visited the school and they duly gyrated to Fat Boy Slim's 'Praise You.' but the audience better understood the scene with Jenny, blank verse and all.

Things were running smoothly but those in the committee were going round with evermore rigid smiles when asked : Where's the band?" as they simply did not know.

Until suddenly the air was rent by the most unmusical

blast -a ship's signal- and round the headland and across the bay, heading for the harbour mouth came a Royal Navy landing craft; it slowed from its full steam ahead until stopping, hitting its marks across the harbour perfectly and as the ramp was lowered, the lights on board came on and the opening bars of Michael and the Angels' greatest hit, "Armageddon" roared forth, live!

They were all there, Gary seated at the back amidst his panoply of drum, Roger, impassive as all good bass players should be, to the right of Michael, Andy, as always to his left, engrossed in his wizardry and Michael to the front with only a microphone between him and the water. This was not the self-effacing Michael of Garden House. His legs were clad in silver , he had on a jacket reminiscent of Roger Daltrey's buckskin from Woodstock, but in white and a simple *bandana corsaire,* black shot through with silver..And in his hands was 'the Sword' .

About twenty years previously, as they were beginning to make it and some money with it, somebody had looked up stuff on the Archangel Michael and had discovered that almost all the paintings had him wielding a sword. So they had contacted one of the great guitar manufacturers who was not too much of a purist and asked if he could, and if he could, whether he would. And the upshot was the Sword, strung like an ordinary guitar, a little awkward to tune but looking like Excalibur from a distance.

For a moment, no-one on land made a sound. It was amazing. And then, for the next hour, they all sang along with all the hits- those that didn't know the words just sang- until Michael carefully handed the Sword over to Spud, his guitar man for twenty years who gave him an acoustic in exchange. He sat and looked at the night sky and then began to pick out a tune. And to sing :

You never asked about them
Those who have been here before
Those who I'd told them I love them
Those I gave a key to my door
You simply took it for granted
Once we had met, I would fall
No more looking for love
In you I'd found my one and all.
One and all, one and all ,one and all one and all

Oh. yes, In you I found my one and all

Then you went and my life went with you
My whole world just fell apart
.Til a little child came and found me
And put back together my heart

And though I didn't know it
Again I was ready to love
Though I tried my best not to show it
Just needed that sign from above
You simply took it for granted
Once again I was ready to fall
No need to go looking for love
Once again I've found my one and all.
One and all, one and all ,one and all one and all
Oh. yes, In you I found my one and all

And all round the harbour, the hundreds of Cornish voices sang the refrain: "One and all, one and all ,one and all one and all, Oh. yes, n you I found my one and all ,

, round and round, time and again, building and building until it became the anthem that the occasion deserved. As the final words rang round the harbour, they were followed by another near silence, although dozens, men as well as women, were in tears. Then the cheers started, and putting down his guitar, Michael dived off the end of the landing craft and swam ashore. Similarly, the other Angels carefully downed tools and joined him in a race to the quay. Mrs Guthrie and Sandy, along with Jake, were standing there, tears filling their eyes, smiles on their faces and big towels in their hands.

"I knew you'd do that, Dad. It was ace. And the song was nice too."

The boy was the first to receive his father's hug but not long after, Rosemarie and Sandy joined him and then the Angels came.

Eventually people started to make their ways home ; Jenny had proudly taken the band and the crew into the pub where they were greeted with more applause, after which Jago and the Mechanicals made a special re-entrance in costume and they too were cheered to the rafters. Then

Jago, pint in hand, wandered out on to the quay to where Michael and Sandy were sitting, the quiet Michael returned.

"Well done, boss," Jago said, holding out his hand. Michael gripped it.

"I hope we were worthy of your hall?"

"Our hall. "

"And very nice it will be, I'm sure." said a sneering voice.

It was Inspector Foot, an apologetic Bert Drake looming behind him.

"Did you enjoy the show, Sergeant?"

"Inspector, sir. I'm sure it was very good but not exactly *.ma tasse de the*' as the French have it. I'm more a brass band man myself. I like a good Souzaphone."

"Andy can play Souzaphone, you know."

"Really?!"

"He can play just about anything. So, you'll be off now?"

"Not exactly,sir. I'm having a raid, sir. Drugs. And I'm glad I have some respectable witnesses. Come on, Constable."

Over his shoulder, Bert mouthed,"Sorry" to them and then followed obediently. Foot stopped at an old cottage on the quay, one of the few that hadn't been done up. It even had smoke going up the chimney rather than underfloor heating or fans.

"I've had my eyes on this establishment for some months. Or to be more correct, nose."And he tapped his nose in his usual manner.

"But-"

"Not now, Constable. Open up!" And, despite the hour, he rapped on the low door. Eventually, the sound of slippered feet approached and the door was opened. By a very old lady.

"Jago! And Mister Michael. And your young lady- how nice. I thought you were very good. I lit the fire as it begins to get chilly this time of year-"

But Foot would not let her finish.

"All right, all right, so where is it?"

"Well, mine's still out the back- never bothered to have it done up cos it's only for me, since my Eric died although there are some quite nice ones, I'm told ,across the harbour but they're not always open."

"What are you talking about?!"

Michael interrupted: "She could well ask you the same."

"Drugs. Drugs, of course. We have information. You can smell it. It's in the air. So where's your cache?!"

Jago tried. "Smell what?"

"I know the smell of cannabis resin when I smell it."

"They don't sell resin no more, mate. Tis all weed. And, unless I'm very much mistake, that's pine resin you'm smellin'. Off the logs. As we all do burn. Could confuse a stupid person."

Foot looked at Jago, then at the fire, then at Michael and Sandy and then the old lady to whom he said: "Scuse me. " He turned on his heel, tucked his swagger stick under his arm and made for the door. As he was about to leave, Cyril's face appeared in the doorway.

"Success? I told you they..." but did not finish as Inspector Foot's swagger stick broke his nose.

"Sorry, auntie," Bert said to the old lady, "But some people just won't listen."

Epilogue

And as the ribbon to the Lady Olivia Vincent and Porthwallow Community Hall was cut jointly by the

Admiral and Michael and they both declared it open, there was a distant but familiar rumble and the cliff top, eaten away by generations of Atlantic breakers smashing up against it, finally gave up the battle royal and slipped gently into the sea two hundred feet below. And engulfed in it went the now-empty White House, thus freeing all its ghosts and releasing all its stories .

Printed in Poland
by Amazon Fulfillment
Poland Sp. z o.o., Wrocław